Crushing

by

TR Simmons

Crushing

Contact Information: info@thewildrosepress.com

Cover Art by *Jennifer Greeff*

The Wild Rose Press, Inc.
PO Box 708
Adams Basin, NY 14410-0708
Visit us at www.thewildrosepress.com

Publishing History
First Edition, 2023
Trade Paperback ISBN 978-1-5092-5110-0
Digital ISBN 978-1-5092-5111-7

Published in the United States of America

There would be thousands of dances taking place in schools tonight. No matter which hemisphere of the planet, Crush-it dances were designated 'dark' events, meaning digital communications were blocked between students. This strategy limited collusion among potential crushers. It also created a primitive state to keep students off balance and force them to adapt. Students sometimes invented elaborate codes and camouflaged them in dance moves to forecast their intentions and strategies with others. Every school did them, but in a crowded room the potential for signals to cross or be misdirected were frequent.

Praise for TR Simmons

"T.R. Simmons' CRUSHING is a provocative teenage dystopian dance opera. In this skewed world, societal conformity is rewarded. Unfortunately, doing what is expected doesn't guarantee happiness, especially when it comes to matters of the heart. Sometimes, the best way to find true love is to break all of the rules."

Diane L Kowalyshyn: Author of, Crossover, Double Cross, Crossbones, Skadegamutch: Monster in the Mirror, Catch .22, Stage Fright

Dedication

To Kyoung-Ju, Roland and Beau. This book would not have been conceived without your passenger seat banter.

Acknowledgements

Special thanks to Diane Kowalyshyn, Magda Gold and Judy Malcolm for suffering through my initial drafts, Johnny Malciw for the polish, and my editor, Ally Robinson for believing in me and this story.

Prologue

Atarah couldn't have been more surprised to see the tall army officer at their door. It took her a split second to realize that a woman's body carried the formal grey uniform. The officer's hair had been cropped to regulation length, but still held a feminine flirt. Atarah's hand naturally reached for the long spans of her own mane for reassurance. She'd grow it to the floor if her mother allowed.

The soldier appeared stiff, shoulders back, eyes straight, only a little sad. "My name is Captain Seneca. May I speak with Min-hee?" A soft voice took the edge off the military presentation.

"You want to speak with my mother?" A brief dizzy spell caught Atarah, but she fought to remain standing. "Is it about my Dad?" She could barely say the words before her mouth went dry. His work had always been top secret. What could have happened?

"You must be Atarah."

"I am."

The captain produced a small brown envelope as if by sleight of hand. "I must give her this letter."

Min-hee, dressed in a green acrobatic leotard arrived from the living room. "What is it? Who's there?"

"It's a soldier. She brought a letter."

Atarah seized her mother's arm for mutual support. Captain Seneca took a deep breath. "I'm sorry to have to bring you this news. You need to know that your husband died yesterday, in the line of duty."

Air squeezed from Atarah's chest. "But he's a quantum biologist. He works in a lab." She blubbered through hot tears.

"Yes. Something went wrong. It was like a bomb hit us. You should know that he died trying to save us all."

"No!" Min-hee shook.

"I'm so sorry. If it is any consolation, I promised him that I would carry on his legacy." The captain held out the letter.

"I will never see him again?" Min-hee sobbed. "Where's his body?"

"You can visit with him through the usual simulation portals the military has arranged with Big Social for grieving families. I hope you will find them therapeutic." The officer placed the letter in Min-hee's shaking hand, saluted, turned on her heel and left.

Chapter One

Six months later.
Monday

"I'm so done."

This mantra had become a ritual for Atarah, not because she wanted to give up on life, but because she held little hope for the coming catastrophe. With five days until her school's annual Crush-it dance desperation had neared perilous levels. If only she could pull the covers over her head and sleep until Saturday.

Atarah sat on the edge of the bed and wiped remnants of drool from her mouth. Sunlight streamed in through a small window making dust and the assortment of sports trophies adorning her room shimmer. With light fingers she ran a vague course over her face in search of underlying blemishes. Would this be a pretty day or a pretty ugly day?

"How many minutes do I have to get to my first class?" she asked.

The wallpaper changed from a rock & roll motif of Jerry Rodriguez contorting with his laser-beam guitar to a satellite's view of her school, Cloverdale High. The number fifty-nine imposed itself over the scene. Smaller numbers adjacent specified the falling seconds. Then came the day's date, Monday February 10, 0026 AI. This was her senior year and a pivotal time in her social ripening.

An orange tabby meandered into the room and jumped up beside her.

"Hello, Carl," Atarah said. "Did Mother send you to get me moving?" She rubbed his fur.

"Good morning, Miss Atarah," the cat said. He sounded like an English butler. "No, she didn't. I am designed to anticipate her whims." Carl blinked his bright green eyes. "You will need to leave your home in thirty minutes if you expect to arrive at school on time. Don't disappoint me." He licked a paw.

Atarah groaned. "It's not possible to disappoint you, Carl. You're a robot." She pressed her nose against his. "You have no feelings and no ghost, you little cutie."

"Indeed. I have no use for a ghost. I can live forever, my dear."

"Touché Carl… touché." Atarah raised her arms and stretched her spine until it cracked. "I want to see outside."

Carl blinked in rapid succession. The small bedroom window expanded into a grand portal from floor to ceiling revealing a view from the forty-second floor of the condo she lived in with her mother. Their building was one of two-dozen skyway condominiums that snaked along the coast. Morning joggers dotted the sandy beach and Great Lakes freighters sunned themselves on the calm water. The world had awoken to a rare cloudless sky. On the surrounding escarpment, windmills spun like regimented giants. Big Social's, gleaming headquarters lorded all things big and small. Solar Zeppelins rode the thermals—sausage shaped balloons with happy faces of whales, elephants, and other animals long extinct.

Atarah slipped from bed and approached her antique full-length mirror, daring a quick glance. Sleek eyes were her best asset. At least that's what her life-long friend Zelina, assured her. The mixing of different races over the decades had destroyed almost all tribal purity. Atarah blended Israeli/Korean on her mother's side with Plains Cree Indian on her father's side. This, along with her five-foot height, made her mind-numbingly forgettable. Bodacious Zelina, on the other hand, embodied exotica—the only genetically true ginger in the entire school. As Head Cheerleader, she'll be mobbed at the Crush-it dance.

She studied the ancient picture postcard slotted into the mirror's frame. A true relic from a more analogue era brought inexplicable comfort to the teen. It depicted a winter scene in a barren wood. The caption read, *Discover the Bruce Trail, Port Hamilton.* Past the leafless birch trees a small stream with snow covered rocks and a fisherman clad in fur posed in the sunny water. Atarah couldn't remember a time she didn't possess the photograph. It had always stirred something inside her. She'd only seen it snow once or twice, but long ago the snow came every year to this part of the world.

Atarah stepped back from the mirror and stripped off her Port Hamilton hockey jersey. Did she have the beauty to survive the upcoming dance? She could be sweet and cute, but in an age of zygote genetics, sweet and cute were the lowest common denominator. With a flip of her short black hair a spicier question came to mind.

"Am I sexy enough?" she said. Her words sounded more like a plea for help than a question for the ages.

"Do tell? Enough for what?" Carl asked. Always the cynic.

"I'm not talking to you." She snatched a brush and threw it at him.

The cat leaped from the bed. "You missed."

She'd never had a boyfriend, although, a Romeo made a move on her as a sophomore. According to her mother, Atarah was too young and he was a first-rate creeper, so she had to turn him down. Athletics, not dates, were her pastime ever since. She glanced around at her trophies. Were they enough to get her noticed by a top school?

This would be her first and only Crush-it and as always AI's Big Social network streamed it world-wide including the Martian colonies. It didn't matter what city you lived in or which school you attend, the format never changed. An AI hologram named Lady Babooshka played master of ceremonies for every dance production. She always wore a gown bejeweled with red hearts. At midnight, when she shouted, 'Crush-it,' everyone ran to their secret crush and revealed their love for them. A kind of madness always followed as students scattered flinging themselves at one another. Big Social posted compilations of these teenage blitzkriegs since they first began over two decades ago. In one case, Atarah remembered watching a handsome Romeo getting mobbed by Juliets until they knocked him to the floor. The scene went viral and universities across the Americas, Europe, and Asia all clamored for him.

Atarah struck some sexy poses in the mirror and contemplated crushing on one of the school's less popular life forms: the gamers and paste eaters or the genetic accidents. Any one of them would be grateful to have her. But it would be risky. Her on-line biorhythms would give her away when her sweat glands didn't authenticate a state of in-loveness. Big Social would put her on the list of Crush-it fakers and she would be trolled for the rest of her life. Better to be listed among those who suicided themselves. Dying for lack of love at least had a smidgen of Shakespeare to it. Short of taking banned drugs to simulate the physical effects of amoré, faking true love in an AI world was impossible.

She took a deep breath. "Carl, play me something hard and heavy by Jerry Rodriguez."

"I should warn you, Miss Atarah, disco is making another comeback." The cat stood on his hind legs and spun around.

"Not today, silly cat. I want to hear "Rip it Off.""

"As you wish," Carl said. He re-composed himself, then blinked three times and the music came to life.

A fast bass jolted Atarah's heart rate and creative powers. She would be dazzling all week at school so any Romeo who had been undecided towards her would have a change of heart. She tore through her closet for her periwinkle steampunk corset with copper buttons. Generally, she reserved fringe fashion for parties, but present circumstances dictated otherwise. She found one of Zelina's School sweaters and paused to smell traces of strawberry in the fabric. The scent momentarily soothed Atarah.

Back on track, Atarah put the sweater down and found what she'd been seeking: leather skirt, pleated with copper panels and matching belt, knee socks, silver army boots, a gear patterned beret to anoint her head and lastly, copper goggles. All designed to provide intrigue and set her apart from the divas, princesses and next-door-Juliets.

The music faded slightly.

"Pardon the interruption my Lady," Carl said. "Your mother has your won-ton soup and toast ready. By the way, the outside temperature is presently twenty-degrees Celsius, more than ten degrees cooler than the average for this time of year. You might consider wearing something warmer."

Atarah slinked into her skirt. It went down to her knees providing a school-respectable length. "You're not my father, Carl. I'll choose what I want to wear."

"Your father is dead," Carl said.

Atarah's heart lurched. "Jeez… I order you to self-destruct." Atarah pulled on her socks.

Silence.

"Your mother would like to know if you want coffee or tea."

"I don't effing know."

She finished buttoning her corset. "Give me lots of mirrors and lots of light and what happened to my music?"

The walls instantly become reflective and the room brightened with light and sound.

"Your pulse rate and blood pressure are much higher than what they should be," Carl shouted. "I hope it's not on my account."

"Shut it. Please and thank you."

Atarah straightened her skirt and pushed bits of cleavage out of her top. "Now you're sugar and spice." Then she grabbed Zelina's Cloverdale sweatshirt from the floor and covered herself to guarantee safe passage to the elevator without a big fight.

"Coming, Mother."

Chapter Two

Cloverdale High School loomed like a large mushroom cloud in the middle of a grassy, sparsely treed twenty-acre campus. The stem, made from gleaming white columns, rose nine floors to its cap, covered in solar-glass energy panels.

Atarah peeled off her sweatshirt to expose her corset. Over two-thousand students attended Cloverdale and she only needed one of them to fall in love with her—not too much to ask.

She crossed the school's threshold and entered the center rotunda, the tech in her biochip engaged the educational mainframe. Nano speakers woven into the building's brickwork nearest her sounded off with a pleasant greeting and a reminder that her first class, creative writing and meditation, would begin in four minutes and twenty-three seconds. She massaged her temples to push away her annoyance of the digital intrusion.

The hallways were well lit with sleek Terrazzo floors and gleaming metallic lockers that zapped her retinas like an interrogator's beam. She slipped on her brass goggles and the world became extra-terrestrial green. The steampunk gear smashed it with peers school-wide as notifications were passed on from her biochip to her mind's eye. As Atarah came into proximity with her locker, it flashed.. It opened with a quick touch. She grabbed her tablet and stuffed the shirt inside, before locking it shut. Her distorted reflection shone in the door's cool metal—like looking through an interdimensional time portal at another Atarah.

Help me, I'm trapped.

****

Creative writing and meditation were her favorite subject. She shared it with Zelina. They sat in recliners next to each other.

"You look peaked, girl-of-mine. Did you get enough sleep last night?" Zelina said. Her chair folded back to fall in line with Atarah's.

Atarah sat up on her elbows. "I assumed I had attained my maximum potential today. Come on, look at my face, not a single blemish." Her confidence slipped. "Tell me why then? When I think I can outshine the world, everyone tells me I'm horrid and when I think I've turned into a goblin, everyone tells me I'm burning down the house… and you've said nothing about my clothes." She couldn't help but notice Zelina's perfection. The black chair accentuated her long strawberry mane and lightly freckled porcelain face. Her tight, school knit sweater with mushroom cloud shamrock crest and pleated skirt revealed all her curves on her six-foot frame. Curvatures Atarah's petite body would never have without the assistance of advanced science.

Zelina smoothed out her skirt. "I'm sorry, I didn't realize you were in such a frayed mood." Her friend made a reassuring smile.

Atarah turned on her side to face Zelina. "I didn't mean to pour rain on you either."

Zelina twirled one of her long braids. "I always love

your clothes—there's so much rhythm in what you wear. I read somewhere; Steampunk has a way of changing you from cute to sexy. You're lucky your mom has connections with the fashionistas in Montreal," Zelina said.

"Take a breath. It's okay. I'm not mad at you."

"Then what's really got your sumptuous eyes all wet? Did Carl-the-Cat make a pass at you or something?"

Atarah laughed. "That wouldn't be the worst thing in the world. At least, I would have an intelligent suiter."

"That's more than what passes for intelligence around here," said Zelina, looking around the room.

"I could hold out for brains, but with the dance this Friday, I don't have time. I need someone to crush on me now," Atarah said. She blinked back emotions to keep her panic from rising. For a teenager, the stakes couldn't be higher. To be loved by someone else is the first step to popularity and acceptance as a contributing member of society. Life-points were awarded by the Big Social network to individuals based on their algorithms for beauty, and online fame. Life-points could be traded for cool clothes, the best computers, and more importantly, access to only the most exclusive university coed utopias on the planet. The alternatives were the military, sweatshops, service worker or worse… and then, who would ever want to be with her?

Zelina's gaze shifted to the chair ahead of them. "Rooco might have a crush on you."

Rooco peered around the back of his chair with spy wear glasses to catch the view up their skirts. Atarah slammed her legs shut. Her cheeks burned. "Rooco, you creeper-turd, mind your own effing business."

"This is my business," he said matter-of-factly as he turned back.

"You see," said Atarah. "Even Rooco has a future, if no one murders him. It may be in peddling lust, but at least he has a future. I have nothing." She threw up her hands. "This is my senior year and all I can expect is to be voted most likely to wear camouflage and see the world."

"But you would sizzle in urban assault gear," Zelina said.

Atarah grinned. "Thanks. When they send me overseas, I'll mail you bullets and trophies from my kills."

"Don't worry, you're not going into the army, if I can help it," Zelina said. "Fact is, it's less than a week before the dance and now you're trying to get noticed. Kind of like cramming for an exam. It is what you do. In the end, you will survive."

"A single crush could do more for my on-line popularity than top marks in Hallmark Philosophy, which I happen to have. I don't have my own cheerleader show with fifty-five million subscribers like you to take me to a top school. You're already set with the best sponsors, financial incentives and rated for super-star nuptials. It doesn't pay to be a short, introverted, female jock." Atarah adjusted the angle of her beret.

"Unless you happened to be a famous introvert," Zelina added.

"It's either that or go crazy."

"Who among us is not crazy or manic? It's only a matter of degrees, girl-of-mine."

The teacher walked into the classroom. "Good morning students."

"Promise me," Atarah whispered. "You'll come to my place after school." She reached over and held her friend's hand. "You can help me brainstorm a strategy for love and riches."

"I'll come after I finish shaking my pom poms at the volleyball game."

Rooco spied around his chair again. "Mind if I come over too?"

Atarah threw her goggles and broke Rooco's glasses in half.

Chapter Three

Yearbook club met at lunch in a bright room with windows overlooking the football field in the school's student club area. Atarah chewed her California rolls slowly, not really tasting the seaweed and rice. Her head leaned against the window. Outside, Zelina directed the cheer squad in their warm ups.

"Earth to Atarah, are you with us?" Darren said. "It's time to get to work."

Atarah turned back to a crowded and cluttered room. The walls displayed a lineage of Cloverdale's past heroes, some of whom were now cultural icons, while others had vanished or were possibly abducted by aliens. Darren and Lizette, the yearbook co-chairs, stood on top of two ancient teacher's desks, while the other worker-bees slouched in formless couches of varying colors and stains.

Darren scanned his tablet notes. "Today is the day we begin to get material and V-paper recordings from all the teams, clubs, cliques, and faculty. Lizette and I matched each of you with four groups to be completed this week. So, everyone, listen for your name. Here are today's assignments."

Atarah had joined the crew in hopes of gaining influence and bonus life-points. The strategy had inherent risks. Naturally, the entire yearbook had to be pure masochism disguised as theatre. Graduates didn't just pose for pictures. The V-paper used to make the book was of high definition and interactive video quality, a requirement guaranteed to provide optimum entertainment. If not, every one of them from Darren and Lizette on down would be socially executed by the senior class.

As Darren continued with his list, the room's giant computer screen scribed his words as he spoke. "Mars, you have the cheerleaders."

Mars pulled his great frame out of his seat with gusto. "Thank you, your royal highnesses, for bestowing this favor upon my head." The only thing Mars liked more than yearbook club was drama class. Out of the nineteen other kids named Mars in the school, he took the prize for most likeable and buffoonish. Publicly, the student body pretended not to care about personal gossip and innuendo, but Mars really didn't.

Atarah turned back to the window. Outside, Zelina and the others were having so much fun laughing and carrying on. "Why can't I cover the Cheerleaders?" Immediately, Atarah regretted her outburst.

Mars gave Atarah his best sad face.

"You can't cover the Cheerleaders; you're too close to Zelina," said Darren.

"What's that supposed to mean?"

"It means we need someone who can be objective," Lizette said. "Besides we have given you a very special assignment."

"Not the school faculty, I hope." She folded her hands preparing to beg.

"No," said Lizette, "that's Starr's assignment."

"Oh, come on, not the teachers. They try too hard." Starr was a lanky button-nosed Spanish or something with blond hair, sitting beside Mars. She buried her face in his big shoulder.

"Actually, Atarah." Lizette's grin grew sly. "Darren and I think you're the only one who can pull this off. We want you to go underground to interview the Unplugged."

"The Unplugged? They're completely counterculture. They have zero on-line presence with Big Social."

"I know," said Lizette, ringing her hands. "They're so analogue. How bizarre is that?"

"Last year they submitted a picture of a middle finger," said Atarah. Needless to say, it didn't make the final cut.

"You can do better. Think of it as an opportunity to earn some double-plus life-points from the Board of Education," Lizette said. She used her enthusiasm like a weapon.

"Why me?"

Lizette's smile turned sour. "Well, if you really need to hear the truth."

Atarah grimaced. "Not really."

"You happen to be the nicest girl in the school," Lizette said.

Everyone in the room nodded, while Atarah imagined all of them with their throats cut. "You know, I'm really not that nice."

"Besides, wearing your tribute-to-Steampunk clothes today shows us that you have foresight and genius," Lizette said. "It's a fashion statement that might speak to the Unplugged in some non-linguistic way." She waved her hands in the air as though she had cast a spell. "One more thing. As we are all keenly aware, the

Crush-it dance is this Friday, and I expect every one of you to attend; especially, if you have someone crushing on you." Lizette gave a knowing glance at Darren; whose face went completely red. "Darren and I will personally interview the college and university scouts in attendance. Next week we'll sift through the social media fallout and cross reference the student body's meta-data in the school computer and then tell stories." Lizette finished her speech looking as though her head would detonate.

Atarah had never witnessed someone loving their life more than Lizette did. She put her hand up to ask a question. "Don't you mean stories about the student body's body-count?"

Lizette scanned the faces before her. "Very clever. We could call it the Crush-it Obituary. What a great idea, Atarah."

Everyone clapped for her.

While Atarah judged whether humanity really deserved to exist, a small earthquake by chance answered this secret contemplation. Atarah pressed against the wall to steady herself. Darren and Lizette remained on top of the desk looking as if they were walking a tightrope. It shook the school for almost ten seconds before settling down. Minor tremors were common enough that no one screamed or freaked out. After the earth quieted, everyone got on with their assigned tasks.

Chapter Four

Atarah secretly idolized the Unplugged at Cloverdale. Like the rockers, clowns and drag queens, the school faculty considered them to be just another harmless counter-culture clique trying to find themselves, but destined to be forgotten. Nevertheless, school authorities did take some preventative measures. No coincidence, all students had to take an introduction to law class on Digital Intransparency Crimes. Atarah had received an A.

Cloverdale's Unplugged hid in plain view like any secret society and rumored to hack and manipulate Big Social with false avatars and aliases in an effort to bring down 'The Machine'. Atarah couldn't be sure how much of this hype could be attributed to urban legend. Biochips were mandatory for high school students. Most students who claimed to be Unplugged were likely wannabes—in it for the mystique. Atarah had met a few in passing, and sometimes wished to be one of them, but didn't really believe she'd ever want to break her biochip connection with Big Social. More importantly, her mother would kill her if she did.

She planned to catch them unawares. They met daily in a small fifty seat rehearsal theatre next to the drama class's set-design room in the sub-basement, where spyware signals couldn't easily penetrate. This worked as a double-shield since most serious Unplugged wore 'dark clothing', clothes that weren't smart, void of tech, which as far as Atarah understood hadn't been criminalized yet. Darren and Lizette gave her a small robot on wheels to boost her recording signal.

Atarah had never been to the lower levels so when the elevator opened to a dark hallway her nerves betrayed her.

"Hello?" Her voice resonated against walls she couldn't see.

She remembered her live feed being carried by the booster-bot at her feet. At least her final minutes of life on Earth would be recorded, a mystery to be uploaded on Big Social where she'd finally attain fame, after the postmortem.

The booster-bot, a spinning crystal ball on wheels, cast light and ghostly shadows on the walls. It ran a signal from Atarah's fiber optic camera and microphone to a central hub upstairs. The signal would carry all the way back to Lizette and Darren, no doubt watching from the comfort of the yearbook club's lounge.

"Bot, go." This simple command made it move ahead of her. As the bot rolled fearlessly down the corridor it triggered motion sensors that lit sections of hallway one by one as they approached large double doors at the end. Atarah's palms grew damp. She was a gifted sweater and could produce great drops of perspiration the instant her anxieties received a kick. She tried to tell herself to be calm, remembering that the Unplugged were not known to be mean. They lived cleaner than most, since they believed drugs were a tool for government control and urban docility. Many were members of Cloverdale's school bands or were stage designers and builders for the theatre troupe. All had an artistic flare, which set Atarah apart from them. She couldn't hold a tune, draw a butterfly or write a love poem and she feared this proclaimed to others she lacked any and all romantic passion.

Atarah checked the camera's fiber strand and microphone wrapped around her ear. It hid along her jawline, almost invisible, unless someone got up close and kissed her, but what were the chances? And anyway, she hadn't come for a date. She needed a yearbook award and the promise of bazillions of life-points.

A mournful electric guitar gushed on the other side. With her hand on the handle, she took a breath. Blueish-green light as if from a thousand fairies fizzed from under the threshold, and skittered on the sheen of her boots.

"Darren, Lizette, I hope you're receiving my feed. I'm about to enter the inner sanctum of the Unplugged." She whispered into her microphone. Darren and Lizette were probably snuggled on a couch, sipping cola and holding hands as though they were on a movie date.

Atarah slipped into the darkened theatre with the robot.

"Stay here," she commanded the bot. Its green glow indicated a strong transmission signal.

One of the school rock bands rehearsed on stage. Dozens of laser floor lights riddled the theatre, painting the air blue. A transgressing array of green light raked up and down the walls as if scanning for extra-terrestrial life. She shielded her eyes every time it passed over her.

Bootleg recordings of an Unplugged band for a school yearbook could earn her thousands of life-points for college or university. "I'm in.".

Atarah made her way down the center aisle, towards

the musicians. The stage lights and reflective costumes were hypnotizing. A well-known reedy Japanese girl, named Mimori played lead guitar. She wore a sleek foil blouse and skirt and moved like a puppet on strings. Her guitar lamented a sad melody as she danced, but this was no solo performance. Mimori's lyrical tones intertwined with a melodious suitor springing from a most unlikely instrument, a musical saw. Whoever imagined a violin bow and a crude saw could be used to make such ethereal resonances? Stoker, that's who. Atarah knew him as an XY distraction from her world religions class.

Stoker sat center stage on an oversized wingback like a king or a devil playing his instrument. He never wore anything with sleeves and had gotten all the best genes from his world-famous parents. A Sudanese father who had won four Olympic gold medals in downhill skiing and a dazzling supermodel/actress Polish mother who loved everyone. Stoker's skin shimmered like warm double-dark chocolate. His contrasting eyes were a genetic marvel, bright and blue. They flashed with the haunting wail summoned from his lashing bow.

Atarah held her breath.

Other band members found a quick beat with drums, bass guitar and shakers.

Stoker began to sing.

"Come like an angel it's only the night

Even when the snows are blowing, we can make it right ...."

His words surfed atop the waves of his bow-saw.

"You say to me that you want to be free,

Damn you girl, why can't you see?

I'm frozen here.

It's only you I need."

Atarah zombied closer to the front as though some magnetic presence held her, until she stood at his feet, drowned in the spectacle. Sound and light flew like pixies to open the box that kept her romantic heart hidden away, but fear and confusion held it closed, keeping her secret safe, even from herself.

The song ended with a crashing minor chord that left the theater in an abrupt silence. Blue luminescence remained thick in the air as though she were being held underwater. Lasers ran stripes over Atarah's body one final time before the meager house lights came on and broke the spell.

"Do we have a new fan?" Stoker put his instrument down. With ease, he jumped off the stage landing beside her. His bare arms and face glistened. "Hey, you're in my religion class, aren't you? Your name is Atarah." He stood more than a foot above her.

Wow, he knew her name. Unbelievable. When had she risen above mere background decoration or a scene extra for the world premiere of Stoker. He actually knew her name. "Yeah, that's right and your name is…." She paused, pretending to try and remember. "Your name is Stoker." She shot him with her finger gun. *Pew.*

He grinned. "You're okay."

Atarah cleared her throat. She found it physically impossible to look away from his sparkling eyes. "So are you." Her words sounded disembodied.

"Hey, I like your clothes," Stoker said. He shoved his hands into his pockets. "Are you part of the Anime Club?"

"Anime? Oh, god no, I'm not…. This is Steampunk."

Stoker stepped back. He seemed to want to take her

all in.

"I like your skin," Atarah blurted.

"What?"

"I mean, I like your band's skins… the drum beat. Your music really burns me." She wiped her brow. "Is it always this hot?"

Again, he gave her a killer smile raising the temperature further. "We practice every day at lunch. You're welcome to come and hang out with us, if you like."

"Really?" Moisture trickled past her temple. "I just might take you up on that offer." She gave him a friendly little punch on a well-developed bicep and shook her hand feigning injury. The other band members remained on stage, putting their instruments away. They didn't seem to be the least bit interested in the time she took with Stoker. The band's three lettered logo hung on chains overhead. "What does D. N. R. mean?" she asked. "Do Nothing Right? Don't Need Rice?" A little inside voice told her to shut up. An ugly chortle flew from her throat. "December, November, Remember?" Perspiration stung her eyes.

"No." Stoker raised his hand.

Atarah could high five him or go for it all. She leaned in to kiss it, but a finger slipped inside her mouth and she gagged a little.

He quickly pulled it back. "Nasty."

"Sorry," she said. "My mistake."

"Never mind." Stoke dried his finger on his pants. "The letters mean, Do-Not-Resuscitate." He sounded a little flustered. "That's the name of our band."

"Do Not Resuscitate? I say that all the time."

Oh God, now he thinks I'm Emo, but at least he let

me kiss his finger, but then I had to go and suck on it.

"How come I've never seen your band at any of the school's concerts?" Atarah asked.

"We're careful to keep away from Big Social. You should come see us perform in one of the off-line clubs. We play most weekends."

She gave her forehead a little smack with her hand. "Oh, that's right, you're Unplugged."

"Atarah…." Stoker's eyes shone like blue moonstones.

She loved it when he spoke her name. Maybe he will ask her to the Crush-it dance or what if he kissed her? She batted her eyes. "Yeah, Stoker."

He touched her arm. She could have sworn an electric charge passed between them. He turned her towards the gallery of seats. "We're all the unplugged, Juliet."

The theatre was full of bemused students staring at her.

Her heart cracked its casing as a little part of her passed away.

Chapter Five

Instead of riding the train after school, Atarah made the forty-five-minute walk home along the boardwalk. The breeze off Lake Ontario always held therapeutic qualities for her. A stiff slap of wind in the face had a way of waking a person.

I'm so done.

She could remember meeting Stoker as something awful and embarrassing or as a great success. Darren and Lizette were over the stars with the rare concert footage of D.N.R. Lucky for her, the Unplugged were unplugged, so there would be no viral embarrassment. They were complete unknowns to the real world of Big Social. Darren and Lizette were more than willing to erase her mortifying conversation with Stoker, which could have been socially fatal. Of course, she'd be in their debt forever.

From now on, she had to be more careful. A similar faux pas with any other clique could not be covered up so easily. In which case, she wouldn't have to worry about the upcoming dance anymore. Very few ever returned to prominence once the trolls of Big Social put their mark on you. They had a way of making a person's total accumulation of life-points worthless, an example of social democracy in its purest form.

Laughter met her as she entered her apartment. She took in the comforting smell of home. The lingering odors of Mother's spicy kimchi never completely vanished. She followed happy echoes along the hallway's black and white checkered panels to the bamboo yoga studio where her mother, Min-hee, performed her famous triple jointed contortions. From the far corner Zelina cartwheeled effortlessly over Min-hee. Both erupted in more laughter.

"Are you two planning on teaming up or something?" A small knot tightened in Atarah's stomach.

Her mother sprang back into human form. "Don't worry, Daughter. I won't take your friend from you."

"Minnie and I were just having some fun while we waited for you." Minnie was Zelina's nickname for her mother.

"I want to steal your friend only for my yoga show. Million more viewers will watch," said Min-hee, in her broken English.

Zelina turned to Atarah. "And your mother can make surprise appearances on my cheerleader show. "She doesn't look a day over twenty-five. She's guaranteed to raise my viewership twenty points with what she can do."

Min-hee scoffed at the compliment.

"I'm surprised you didn't think of this idea before." Atarah backed out of the room. "Don't let me interrupt. I have homework to do."

Atarah ran to her bedroom, sliding the door shut before heaving a great emotional sigh. She looked in her mirror. Why did she expect life to be fair? Everyone around her encapsulated beauty and talent, while she remained suspended in a world of averageness. Her fingers touched the old postcard still held to the mirror's frame and made a wish.

It didn't take long before a quiet knock rapped. Atarah checked to make sure her eyes were dry. "Come in," she said. Her fists clenched, straining to find a cheery voice.

Zelina stepped in, flushed and dejected.

Atarah put her entire force of being into keeping her feelings tied in a knot. She feared that if she moved even a finger, they would all spill.

Zelina didn't hesitate, but took her into her bosom, holding her as if she'd never let go. "I'm sorry, Atarah. I know you're struggling right now. I'd rather die than hurt you."

Atarah sniffled. "It's just a raw time for me, with the dance and everything, so I'm a little bit sensitive. I know I should be on fire for the both of you."

"You'll find your place. I know you will. In the meantime, I would love it if you could be on my show."

"Thanks, but I don't want your pity. Well, maybe a little bit."

Zelina gave her a broad smile. "Sure you do, girl-of-mine. Besides we could use your smallness to practice throwing and catching. Do you bounce?"

Atarah looked into the face of her much taller friend. "I am quite bouncy."

"In this world, we do what it takes to not get ignored. Your size is seen as a disability, so you must work harder than everyone else to stay even. Nothing is going to change that, including pity." Zelina put both hands on Atarah's shoulders. "Minnie is waiting for us in the kitchen with what I'm sure will be some strange and magical tea. If the three of us put our superior female brains together we can come up with a plan for the dance and your future popularity."

"They are one-and-the-same, I'm afraid," Atarah said.

Tea was Min-hee's solution to every problem. She sat at the small round kitchen table in the lotus position cupping her hot drink with both hands. The two girls took their own chairs. Their drinks cooled in small clay crockery on bamboo place settings.

"Take a sip, daughter. The liquid will soothe your chakras. Make you grounded."

"Thanks, mom, but what I really need is for someone to fall in love with me before Friday."

"Don't be silly. You can't force it. The night I met your father neither one of us were looking to fall in love. "Love found us after all."

"That's so romantic, Minnie," said Zelina.

""Love Found Us After All" is the name of a song." Atarah rolled her eyes. "That's not original, and besides, love always seems to find you, Zelina. Let's count them. Six different football players, all with awesome hair, since your freshmen year. I think your present Romeo, Marc, is the nicest one of the bunch." She gave her friend a knowing smile. "And what are the odds none of them had a handsome single friend for double dates?" She sat back and crossed her arms.

"It's high school's natural selection," Zelina said. "Football players date cheerleaders and cheerleaders date football players."

"How cliché," Atarah said.

"Football players are not your type, daughter," said Min-hee.

A white cylindrical cleaning-bot stood with its four arms resting at its side next to the stove. Atarah had attached a picture of Jerry Rodriquez's wounded guitar-solo face on the bot's head.

Zelina pointed to it. "Jerry Rodriquez is your type. You're always asking why things have to be the way they are. Jerry always asks why in his lyrics too."

Min-hee shrieked. "Is he man or woman? I can't tell. He's so ugly."

"Mother. Be nice. I happen to think he's beautiful."

"Good, you can marry the robot. At least you won't have to do any of the house vacuuming."

They all laughed.

"I know, I need to lighten-up and let it happen," said Atarah. "I actually did meet someone today. Totally crushable."

"This is news, girl-of-mine." Zelina pressed in close to her friend.

"I had to get an interview with the Unplugged for yearbook. I caught Do Not Resuscitate doing their lunch-time rehearsal."

"You recorded them? They don't let any of their performances on Big Social. It's what makes them legendary."

"Well, I managed to record a small part of one of their songs, but just for the yearbook. Their music really burned my ghost. After they finished playing, Stoker talked to me… and he knew me by name. He's very good-looking and nice."

Zelina flushed. "Really?"

"Yeah, are you okay?"

Zelina choked. "I'm fine."

"I mean it. Stoker is really nice. Not the least bit pretentious. I hoped for a brief minute, he might ask me to the dance."

Carl pounced into the room swishing his tail. "I'm sorry to interrupt your insufferable conversation ladies," he said. "According to my calculations, Zelina's blood pressure and heart rate have risen to dangerous levels. Should I call for medical assistance?"

Atarah took Zelina's hand. "What's wrong? Let me feel your forehead."

Min-hee ran to the sink to get a glass of water.

"I'm fine. Truly, I am. It's probably nothing. I happened to remember I've got to cram for a geography test on rising sea levels. It's worth half my grade."

Atarah studied her friend. "Are you jealous? Are you sparking for Stoker?"

"No, of course not. Marc is my boyfriend. We love each other."

"Stoker is all yours if you want him." Atarah fell back in her chair. "You don't have to worry about me."

"What do you mean?"

Once again, Atarah pushed her feelings away. "As quickly as the fire caught for us, I foolishly gave him a cold shower."

"Zelina's biorhythms have normalized," Carl announced. "I recommend that she consults medical advice should her distress return." He flopped down in the middle of the kitchen floor. "On the other hand, Atarah's are now elevated, but I have come to expect that on any given day." He gave his paws a nonchalant lick.

Atarah stood. "Whenever I talk to a Romeo my brain turns off. Why am I so intimidated?"

"Listen, daughter," Min-hee pressed her hands into the front of her chair and lifted her bottom from the seat as her legs stretched out on either side. "You need to balance your life with the past, present and future."

Slowly, she lifted her legs until her feet were behind her ears. "Everything is more complicated when you're young. Because you live in the present, whatever happens to you is magnified. You never imagine tomorrow can be better or different."

"But Mom, the dance is Friday," Atarah said. She paced.

Carl exited the room to avoid being stepped on.

Min-hee returned to a polite sitting position. "Join us at the table, Atarah. There is something you both need to understand."

"I don't want to sit down."

Min-hee gave her daughter a stern look.

Atarah plunked down.

Min-hee continued. "Having a Romeo is not better or worse. He can ruin your social reputation as much as he can enhance it, while your impact on him is minimal." Min-hee took the hands of both girls. "Even Zelina must be careful and choose wisely. She is just beginning her fame, and it can easily be taken away from her with one false step."

"What are you saying, Mom?"

"No one is completely secure when everyone is watching, and this is even more true when you are young. Sometimes it is good to have nothing to lose. Let things happen naturally. It is okay to be afraid and unsure, if you also have hope. Hope and fear are always partnered. No way around it."

"Easy for you to say. You're popular. You have millions of people all over the world watching your yoga show." Atarah resumed drinking her tea. "What I don't understand is that you're as short as me, but you're still accepted."

"Love and popularity are not the only way. They happen to be the easy way for some," Min-hee said. "I compensate for my shortness by being triple jointed. I'm seen as an anomaly, so my smallness is overlooked."

"You mean you're seen as a freak, so you're forgiven for not being like most people," Atarah said.

"It is the way of things," Min-hee said. She appeared a little dejected. "For now, it is important to finish high school and gain more life-points to keep you out of the army. I already lost your father to one war. I wouldn't survive if I lost you to another."

"How come I didn't get any of Dad's tallness?"

"I wonder that myself. A man so tall should have given something to you. That is why we didn't enquire to have your genes manipulated."

Atarah rubbed her temples. "If I can get one person to crush on me at the dance, I could earn anywhere from a thousand to ten times that much if he happens to be someone with a lot of popularity. I could reject him and still be catapulted into a top college." She took another sip of her tea. "But I would much rather fall in love."

"I wish we lived in a world where love and popularity were not something people traded for things," Zelina said.

"Hasn't it always been this way?" Atarah asked.

Min-hee shook her head. "Both of you, remember what I say, because it is truth. I learned from my husband—love cannot be forced. Not if it is real. It comes to you or it does not, like an unbridled horse. It will run to whomever it desires. It cannot be stopped... and if you try and stop it, someone always gets hurt."

"That's why you need to be yourself," said Zelina.

"I am myself. That's the problem."

"No, you haven't been." Zelina took a turn pacing the floor. "For the last few weeks, you've tried on more clothes and personalities than a runway model. You're a tomboy, a jock-girl. You play field hockey, ice hockey, volleyball, baseball, basketball and just about every sport invented. You're a Taekwondo black belt and you can run for hours without stopping. You have talent and you will find a way to turn that talent into life-points. You don't need to sell your love to some guy who's only interested in accumulating life-points from you—use what you have. Maybe something unexpected will happen. In the meantime, just be your usual, overheated, dramatic, tomboy self. I love that person more than you can imagine."

"So, what you're saying is, tomorrow I should show off my butt in tight athletic wear?"

"I wanted to be deeper than that, but I suppose it couldn't hurt," Zelina said.

Atarah raised her teacup. "Here's to leggings."

Chapter Six

Tuesday

Another sunny day renewed Atarah's optimism. Her confidence sored in Min-hee's branded black yoga pants, cropped Port Hamilton hockey jersey, and white high-tops on her feet. A thin headband gave her short hair a slight lift.

Round, mirrored sunglasses held back the brightness of the school's hallways as she jogged to her first class, World Religions. She wanted to get there early to avoid Stoker. If she took the farthest seat, he wouldn't have to walk past her. Avoiding embarrassment took planning and effort.

"Dark glasses off please, Atarah," her teacher, Mr. Swain said.

They're mirrored, not dark.

He stood at the classroom's entrance dressed in a blue suit and in his usual at ease stance—both hands behind his back. "You're ahead of your time, this morning." He was a tall rigid man with a back comprised of wooden planks.

"Yes, sir." She had to stop herself from saluting. "I jogged to school today."

"Very good. Try and make it a habit, would you?"

"Will do, sir." Atarah slipped past him and cruised into the classroom. The school's computer congratulated her on being on time. Only, someone else had arrived before her. Stoker had claimed a desk on the far side.

Paralyzing fluid flooded her veins. Stoker glanced over from his tablet, before quickly looking back down, only to raise his head again. Atarah realized the flaw in her strategy and wished she'd come late to class.

Without elegance or grace, Atarah broke free from her paralysis and lunged into a front seat. She could feel his eyes on the back of her head. He might as well be sitting directly behind her.

"Hello, Atarah."

Atarah jumped like a cat from her chair. Somehow, Stoker had stealthily moved to the desk behind her.

He raised his hands. "Sorry, I didn't mean to scare you." His smile returned. "I only wanted to say hi." He blinked his genetically engineered blue charms.

But she wasn't ready to sit back down. Instead, her hands held her hips and she cocked her head. "You got something in your eyes?"

His dark pigment blushed as though he were radiating a burn. "I wanted to apologize to you about yesterday. Didn't mean to embarrass you in front of everybody."

"You didn't embarrass me." Her posture became awkward, so she returned to her desk, swiveling her chair so they could talk face to face. "I embarrassed myself. I never need any help in that department. It's one of my special talents." Predictably, her own temperature began to rise as her glands turned on the taps.

He studied her face. "Are you coming from a workout?"

"No, I often dress like this. I like sports—bit of a tomboy, I guess. At least that's what Zelina calls me."

She shrugged. "That's my thing."

"Yeah, I know that. What I mean is that you're really perspiring." He pulled out a neatly folded red bandana from his back pocket. "Here, use this."

"Sure, thanks." She took it and wiped down her face. "Besides embarrassing myself, my body tends to dampen a lot… and when I say, a lot… I mean, a lot."

Shit.

A small laugh escaped Stoker. "You're funny."

"Good funny or stupid kind of funny?"

"Funny is funny, it's all good to me."

"Okay, then." She looked at him sideways.

"Time to begin our class," said Mr. Swain, as he shut the door.

Bewildered, Atarah never realized the classroom had filled with students. She locked-on to her teacher, and no longer minded Stoker's eyes looking at the back of her head. His bandana went straight into her pocket for good luck.

Chapter Seven

Lunchtime came and Atarah bid adieu to Stoker and headed for the yearbook room to receive today's orders. She walked with a slight skip to her step, buoyed by the prospect of romance with Stoker, although, secretly almost any romance would do. The time had come to put away her fears of a serious relationship. Stoker might have never been on her lover's radar, but like her mother said, 'love is a galloping horse' or something like that. They didn't have much in common, but who cares, so long as he's handsome and talented. She wanted to find a way to unplug him from the Unplugged and go main-stream. A feat so rare, it could easily rocket her to Big Social stardom. Maybe the very act of filming his group would help him to see the futility of it all. Could love and fame come together with a guy like Stoker? He'd thank her for the video. Probably hire her to be their band's promoter. It didn't make sense keeping themselves a secret from Big Social sponsorship. They were doing nothing to advertise their music, let alone change the world.

Ahead, Zelina and Marc walked hand in hand. Something stirred inside. Atarah had been best friends with Zelina since kindergarten and they shared an inseparable bond ever since. Only problem, boys kept getting in the way. She ran between them, pulling their hands apart. "Hey you two, how's everything?"

"We're on our way to shoot another *Zelina, the Red Headed Cheerleader* episode. Marc is going to be my athlete of the week. Do you want to come? I can always use you," Zelina said. Her eyes grew wide and hopeful.

"You'll toss me around like a football, then leave me discarded in some corner like a forgotten birthday present." Atarah pouted her lips. "Besides, I have far more important work to accomplish over lunch."

"You mean like finding clues to an old Cloverdale crime mystery that happened fifty years ago?" Marc said. He gave her a little wink.

Atarah liked Marc even if he did get between her and Zelina. Lighthearted and friendly, he always tried to make people feel good, however, his affinity for winking made Atarah uncomfortable. She diagnosed it as a personality flaw, like a limp handshake.

"Mars came to our practice yesterday," said Zelina. "He did an expose on my squad and then a personal interview with my heartthrob boyfriend."

"That's nice." Atarah took a hard, serious look at Marc. "Remember, I've known her longer than you, and I know all her secrets." Then, she threw a deliberate wink right back at him.

"Not all of them, I hope," he said. Then he had the audacity to return the wink, plus two.

"Enough, you two weirdos." Zelina took Marc's hand and pulled him closer. "Tell me, Atarah, how's your day going? Better than yesterday, I hope."

"A lot better, but I need to go. I don't want to keep Lizette and Darren waiting."

"Okay, sure. But first, did you manage to avoid Mr. Unplugged in World Religions class?"

"Stoker? Well, he kind of came on to me, I think."

She unzipped her pocket and took out his bandana. "He gave me this to wipe the sweat off my face. Isn't that great?"

Zelina looked gob smacked.

"We might have something after all." Atarah shrugged. "Anyway, got to run. See you later."

Cheerleaders were not the only Juliets with the ability to pick up Romeos. Stoker could be seen as quite the prize too and garner her more life-points than all of Zelina's football playing boyfriends combined. No longer being the third-wheel would redefine their relationship for the better.

Atarah burst into the yearbook lounge as Lizette and Darren were climbing on their command desks to give out the lunch-time tasks.

"Three cheers for Atarah," Darren said.

Atarah stopped as the door gave her back-end a little help into the room. The place erupted with praise.

"What's going on?" she asked. Everyone returned to their seats.

"Your recording of D.N.R. was brilliant and could help catapult us into the top three of all-time best yearbooks," Lizette said. She held three fingers up.

"Wow," Atarah said.

"Yeah, you're the best." Darren winked.

It took a second for this unexpected eye signal to reach Atarah's cognitive brain center. First Marc and now Darren. What were the odds? Could it have been a misfired blink that became a wink? If it were deliberate, what could it mean? Keep up the good work? You are a socially viable person at this school? Or maybe something much more?

Lizette began to read off her list of assignments.

Mars got the fun-loving clown club. He clapped with excitement. "Yesterday they made me an honorary cheerleader. Maybe the clowns will make me one of them. Wouldn't that be great?"

He is exhausting.

"And next we come to Atarah," Lizette said. "You have the privilege of interviewing The League of Neo-Feminists."

Another trial by fire, she mused.

Atarah believed she could be as feminist as the next person, her mother would expect nothing less from her, and she would expect nothing less from herself, but was she feminist enough for The League? They could be intimidating. Anyone could tell who were active members, because they carried blood red parasols. Regular parasols depicted flowers and animals or Renaissance art. Like the suffragettes of old, The League didn't use their mini umbrellas to only keep the sun off their skin. They were weapons against anyone standing against gender equality. Cloverdale had one of the most popular Leagues in Port Hamilton, famous for cutting-edge ideas and their most eccentric leader, Mia. They enjoyed an unprecedented level of emancipation from their teachers, due to the fact their message had a way of recruiting other students from outside the district to attend Cloverdale.

The League of Feminists operated from Amazon Island which happened to be the room immediately across the hall from the yearbook club room. Scribed on the entrance to their inner sanctum were the words, *Only feminists may cross this threshold without fear.* Atarah knocked and within a jiffy the gateway to Amazon Island opened on shrill hinges.

A freshman boy, smaller than herself, with tanned skin and eyes too big for his head, greeted her.

"May I help you?" he said. He wore a red long-sleeved shirt with an insignia to indicate he ranked with security.

Confusion made Atarah hesitate. She looked past the boy to a sterile anteroom that could have belonged to a dentist's office. "Well, I'm with the yearbook crew and wanted to speak with Mia for the upcoming edition."

"Are you part of the school's faculty?"

"No, I'm a senior. Do I look that old to you?"

"Beg your pardon, but I've been instructed to ask specific questions."

"What questions?"

He shifted his stance. "Are you a feminist?"

"Are you?"

"Of course." He tried to look taller. "I am or I wouldn't be Tuesday's Gate-Keeper-to-the-Island."

"Tuesday?"

"Yes, someone else will be standing guard on Wednesday."

"Okay then, yes, I'm a feminist." Atarah raised her right hand and gave the boy a Vulcan greeting.

A great smile radiated from his face. "Please come in, Sister."

"Thank you." The little room had eight office chairs and a table with an assortment of interactive magazines about fashion, art, and mechanical engineering. Interactive posters of women of leadership adorned the walls. Signs with overt political statements were smattered between them. One depicted a red circle with a diagonal line running through it superimposed over the word 'slut' and another over the word 'bitch.' Atarah winced.

The boy tugged at her arm. "What is your name, Sister?"

"Atarah," she said.

"Please come with me, Sister Atarah."

He took her down a hallway to an enormous film set, complete with lights, camera, and backdrop of a tropical beach. Enough sand had been spread about to have a proper volleyball game. In the middle of it all, a little grass hut baked under stage lights. A mix of students prepared equipment and props without paying any mind to her. Atarah recognized Mia absorbed with her tablet as she came from behind the hut wearing an Amazonian battle costume: golden breast plate, pleated-armor skirt, sandals, and sword.

"Sister Mia is reviewing her script for this afternoon's show. Feel free to record as you wish," he said. "I'll let the Queen know you're here."

Atarah panned her camera to take in the full view before narrowing in on a couple of Romeos sitting on a bench kissing. Her palms began to perspire and she stopped filming. Hopefully, Big Social didn't see them or they might lose all of their life-points. Could Mia's Island be a true oasis separate from Big Social? No one could argue, Mia had a revolutionary's heart and believed everyone could be a feminist, by choice and degree.

Atarah refocused, checked her camera and microphone filament wired around her ear. Why were her hands shaking so?

Tuesday's Gate-Keeper approached Mia and spoke to her. Mia immediately looked across the room and waved Atarah over. "It's a pleasure to have someone from yearbook club visit us." Mia injected electricity into everything. At well over six feet, the Queen met all the physical Amazonian requirements—broad shoulders, red-colored fingernails, thighs capable of snapping the necks of unenlightened menfolk. She gave Atarah a real hug, pressing the stiff fabric breastplate of her golden armor into Atarah's face. "Don't let your tiny stature preclude you from being an Amazonian feminist. So long as your heart sings our message you can be ten-feet-tall." Mia's fine white skin might have never seen the sun. Set against her full red lips and perfect teeth, it was impossible for Atarah not to be seduced by every syllable her vast mouth proclaimed.

"Thanks," Atarah said. "Would you mind if I record an interview with you for the yearbook?" Her whole body trembled. What had come over her?

"Would I mind?" Mia tipped her head back and laughed uproariously exposing her uvula to the lighting crew. "I wouldn't be Queen of the Island if I didn't want publicity."

"Majesty," Atarah gave a slight curtsy. "Besides, if we women don't help each other, who will?"

"That's a very simple truth," Mia said. She led Atarah to a couple of green directors' chairs positioned in front of the hut. "Why don't we use this as our backdrop for the interview? Isn't it lovely? I persuaded the Unplugged set designers to make it for me."

A pang of jealousy nipped at Atarah. What might Stoker do in Mia's clutches. She shook off these feelings knowing Stoker would just build her the damn hut and nothing more.

Atarah waited for the Queen to sit first, then followed suit.

"Last year you were voted president of the League of Neo-Feminists for Cloverdale," Atarah said.

"You might say, I battled my predecessor for the job and won—overwhelmingly victorious."

"One of your first acts as president… I mean queen was to launch the Amazonian Island concept on Big Social."

"We are no longer a league, but a monarchy, and I am Queen. I invited Big Social to spread our message on my terms. Otherwise, I don't want it anywhere near my island."

"I see."

"Don't misunderstand, I haven't taken away suffrage for our members or anything like that." She waved her hand to scoff at the idea.

"To do so would be more than a little ironic," Atarah said. She should have rehearsed some questions first.

"Indeed, our former trail blazers fought hard for the right to vote and own land. Now it is my job to proclaim the new feminism on their behalf."

"And what is the new feminism?" Atarah asked.

Everyone on the island stopped in their tracks.

Mia appeared bewildered, even speechless.

Atarah shifted to the edge of her chair. "Who do women have to slap in the face to finally have women and men live more harmoniously? Big Social? Each other?" Atarah asked.

Mia's face reddened. "Atarah, you are an inspiration." Crewmembers ran to their stations. Lights brightened. A fan blew fake sea air, flipping Atarah's hair and drying her lips.

"Good question, Atarah. I had never expressed it that way before. Who do we have to slap in the face to share in gender equality?"

The sound of waves and the periodic squawk of a digital seagull punctuated the visual effects to complete Mia's tropical fantasy.

"Feminism is a state of being, Sister. It is not a club or a league or place that exists in a dimensional universe. Feminism is a crown we all share, a matriarchal monarchy and world unto itself." Mia stood and faced the cameras. "We don't need the masculine gender to give us value or equality for harmony to exist. And the last thing we need is Big Social's appraisal on our minds and bodies. Instead, we must give it to ourselves, and to each other. Male entitlements exists because they give each other permission to have them. Good on them. But we women, don't always do that for each other. Like the 'old boy's clubs' it's time the women form our own 'old girls clubs'."

"Instead of whisky we'll be drinking mojitos," Atarah added. With the realization she had been forgotten in all of Mia's zealousness, Atarah vacated her chair and moved to the periphery. She needed to record this experience full-on. Without a doubt, this Queen would go places. Even though she rubbed against the traditional thinking of Big Social, Mia had the formula for fame and fortune and who couldn't fall in love with that?

Mia looked ready to combust. "My new sister-friend Atarah has inspired me with her words of action. She said, 'who do we have to slap in the face to make women and men live more harmoniously?'" Mia pointed at Atarah. "You truly do have a heart of an Amazonian warrior."

Every camera turned to meet Atarah. She gave a shy

wave back at them while beads of water trickled down her temples. Only when the attention moved back to Mia did she take a breath.

"Women have been asking men for equality for hundreds of years," Mia continued. "Well, they are not going to give it to us, for it is not theirs to give. They don't have it. We must take it for ourselves and from ourselves. We must give it to each other." Mia drew her authentic looking sword. "Today, Sisters, we must stop putting one another down. We must stop calling each other names, like slut, bitch and whore-lock. It distorts our human value when it is done to win the approval of others or Big Social's popularity game. These swear words have no equal for men. Men don't have to put us down, we do it to ourselves, and they stand back in complete amusement when we do. The AI networks promote this behavior when they give more life-points for behavior that dominates others in the name of happiness. Screw that, Big Social."

Mia's speech began to stir something inside of Atarah. Women were constantly belittling each other to rise higher in Big Social's popularity game. Shame filled her. To think, she had done it on more than one occasion. Examples riddled the Big Social networks all over the world.

Mia returned her sword to its sleeve. "I would like to proclaim that our crusade will now move into a new, more active phase." She planted her feet in the sand and placed both hands on her chest plate. A broad smile brightened her demeanor. "I call it the slap-them-in-the-face educational network. Warriors, get to your printers and make yourself a white glove. Keep it with you always. If ever another woman calls you a derogatory name or tries to belittle you, in the name of self-empowerment, it is your Amazonian duty to use your glove of honor to slap her in the face." Mia mimed a slap. "Not too hard of course, we don't want to leave a mark, some of us have delicate skin. Just enough to knock some sense into her double X chromosomes. In the age of chivalry, men protected a woman's honor in this way. Sometimes they resorted to pistols at dawn." Mia pointed a finger. "Now, we must do it for ourselves."

The camera lights turned red and Mia slid back into her director chair fanning her afterglow.

Atarah joined her. "You were amazing." She took Stoker's bandana and without compulsion, dabbed the Amazon Queen's brow.

"Thank you, Atarah. I hadn't expected to say most of that. It just poured out and I have you to thank. What you said… how you said it, so simply. Women must change the way we treat each other. The answer in a few simple words, but we have been deaf to its siren call."

"It's an honor to be your inspiration." Atarah now wiped her own forehead. "But tell me one thing, how does falling in love play into all this for you?"

"For me, personally? I'm like everyone else. I'm looking for love, not power. I know that sounds funny coming from the Queen. But I've learned the hard way. Empowerment over others is the wrong way to get recognition. Makes us all assholes, eventually. We all need someone to love and to love us in return. A couple needs to bring the best out of each other." Mia leaned over and gently kissed Atarah's lips. "You for example, might make me very happy, if it weren't for the fact you're already spoken for. That's right, you have a secret admirer at this school."

Atarah pulled back, the kiss all but forgotten. "What do you mean? I'm not spoken for." She touched her mouth with her finger.

Mia gave another throaty laugh. And leaned in for another try. "You protect your heart too much. Maybe if you shut your eyes, you'll understand that love is much closer than you imagined."

With more than a little trepidation, Atarah closed her eyes and readied her lips. It began with Mia's tender touch and grew with intensity as her probing woke the rest of her body. Finally, Mia relented, leaving Atarah without words for poems or proclamations, only the desire for more.

Mia gazed at her—absently biting her bottom lip.

"Wow." Atarah could only manage a whisper. "You sure don't kiss like my grandmother. I never expected my first kiss would come from another…."

"Life is nothing, if it is not a little ironic. We live in two worlds, sister." Mia placed a hand on Atarah's knee. "There is the world we perceive around us, and then there is a truer world behind it. Irony happens when they collide. If you can remember my kiss, you'll know true love when it comes for you."

With a gentle hand, Tuesday's Gate-Keeper delicately escorted a very wobbly Atarah off the island.

Chapter Eight

After school, Atarah joined Zelina and Marc sailing on Lake Ontario. The temperature had warmed to thirty-six degrees Celsius and the wind whipped steadily. Zelina's show sponsor, Fantasy Boats and Dories, had given her full use of a forty-foot Sloop sailboat. The company allowed it to be christened, "Cheers," with the proviso she promoted their brand on her cheerleading show. Atarah held the camera while 'super couple'— Zelina and Marc—posed and performed action shots with zinc covered noses and high fashion swimwear. Later they would add cheesy guitar riffs and playful emojis.

When they were finished filming, Marc set the boat's computer to beat a course along the shoreline. Zelina grabbed her robe and a big floppy hat. She often remarked she could feel herself age by just thinking about the sun on her skin. Atarah's lineage handled the solar elements better. She still used SPF 120 as a block and didn't see the need to cover herself.

Marc kept watch from the helm for traffic even though the boat had the most modern automatic avoidance systems.

Zelina returned from below and handed him a cola. "Your poses were very manly today, Romeo." She gave him a long kiss on the mouth. "This shoot could turn out to be one of our best vids. Right Atarah?"

Atarah sat with her legs resting along the bench beside the helm pretending to be reviewing her camera footage, but really thinking about Mia. "I went to Amazon Island today."

"So, you met Queen Mia," Zelina plunked down on the seat next to Atarah's feet.

"The mad queen," Marc added.

"She's mad, for sure, but I love her fearlessness," said Zelina.

"Yeah, slap them in the face, right?" Atarah said.

They all laughed.

"Mia told me I had inspired her with the idea," Atarah said. "I'm not entirely sure I want any of the credit."

"I never did take you for a revolutionary," Marc said.

"It won't catch on. The idea is from another century," Atarah said. "We'll all have to wear gloves and say things like, 'you cad' and 'I must protect my honor or it will be slaps-in-the-face at dawn'."

"I'd like it if it did have some effect." Zelina said. "I hate being called slut, especially by other women."

"They're jealous because you're so rich and beautiful," Marc leaned over and gave her a squeeze.

Atarah sat straight. "You think you could, do it?"

"Do what?"

"Slap someone." Atarah whacked the thin air with her hand. "A solid kick in the face might be more impactful."

"Maybe." Zelina hesitated. "Probably. I would be more likely to participate if others were doing it too."

"It ain't no revolution if no one gets their nose bloodied," Marc said. He gave Atarah a wink.

Atarah couldn't help but look away. "The water is so beautiful today." Her condominium stood on shore; a regimented soldier dressed in golden armor. A Zeppelin moved slowly past it casting a shadow and changing its gold finish to dingy grey. "Beauty never lasts does it?"

"It does if you can afford to pay for it," Zelina said.

"Min-hee told me there was a time when doing sexy video shoots of seventeen-year-olds would have been grounds for getting yourself locked in your bedroom without dinner."

"Not anymore. Fame comes at any price for any age now." Zelina appeared a little wistful.

"Does it ever bother you to be an object of beauty?" Atarah asked. "To always be objectified as sexy?"

"Would it bother you?" Zelina returned the question. "It's been my persona since I was fourteen. My parents encouraged me and put me in pageantry vids. I wouldn't have it any other way. At least not in this world. The alternatives are too depressing." She started to bite a fingernail, then caught herself.

"Yes, but wouldn't you want people to get to know you for things other than…."

"My big boobs."

"Amen," Marc said.

"That's what I mean," said Atarah. "Careful Marc, I might have to slap you in the face."

Zelina stood. "I don't believe there is anybody who doesn't want to feel attractive and sexy to other people." She stood, opened her robe, and briefly flashed her bikini clad body to Atarah. "We all want to be an object of beauty to somebody."

Atarah cheeks warmed. "But all the time? To everybody?"

"Yes, all the time and at least to those who matter to me." Zelina hugged Marc from behind.

"Don't you want people to see you for being smart or nice?" Atarah asked.

"Who needs to be smart when we have AI," Marc said. "Nice is good though. It's a part of being beautiful. Makes a person that much more desirable. You and Zelina are a couple of the nicest people I know. So, to me you're both just as beautiful even though you have very different bodies."

I'll tell you what makes me worry." Zelina let go of Marc. "I worry more after the fact. After they get to kiss you and touch you."

"What do you mean?" Atarah asked.

"Yeah, what do you mean?" Marc said.

"Think of yourself as a work-of-art: a painting, like a Renoir or Tom Thompson."

"Get over yourself, Zelina," Marc said. "You're more of a Picasso. All mixed up."

"Shut it, Romeo." Zelina continued undeterred. She moved in close beside Atarah. "It's a paradox. Big Social has cast me as a beautiful person, so people treat me as some kind of art treasure. I should know. People are shameless when they see me. They stare and talk, but most of all they want to touch me. And like with a fine painting, if I'm touched by even a finger, part of them, the oils on their skin for example become part of me-the-painting and the impurities begin a process of change. That's when I worry. I don't want to be made into someone I'm not in order to have the world touch me."

"Jeez, Zelina that's really twisted," Marc said.

"But you're not a painting, an inanimate thing or property that can be owned," Atarah said. "A person with a strong sense of themselves can't be so easily damaged," Atarah said. "We can change on our own terms."

Zelina put an arm around Atarah. "Maybe you're right, girl-of-mine. All I know, is what you and I have is real. The rest is just a big show."

"Hey, I should be offended," Marc said. "Do you think of me as merely some chiseled stone? A kind of glorious representation of beauty in all its maleness?" He ran a finger along his jaw line.

Atarah let a giggle escape.

"Yes, Marc you're my Adonis. I love that you're a great kisser." Zelina turned to Atarah and gave her a knowing smile. "That's got to count for something."

It warmed Atarah to know that her friendship with Zelina remained authentic.

As the sun began to set, they reached the dock. Atarah tied off the bow line, while Zelina took care of the stern. After securing the boat, they put their school clothes back on and climbed the steps to the boardwalk in time to see a woman slap another woman in the face with a white glove. "I'm not the bitch." Some of the onlookers clapped. "Don't you dare call me that again," the offended woman said.

"This can't be happening," Marc said. He absentmindedly rubbed his own cheek.

"Well, I guess it's official," Atarah said. "It took about seven hours for Mia's revolution to go viral."

Chapter Nine

During dinner, Min-hee reminisced with Atarah about her father. They looked through a few family albums. The V-paper could make Atarah believe he still lived.

Later that night, sleep didn't come easily for Atarah. The more she chased after it the more elusive it became. The clock glowed green 2:01 am. Her stomach roiled with sushi, spicy dumplings, and worry. She wanted to run. She wanted to kick. Anything to make her stop thinking.

Atarah flopped to the floor. The shock of landing brought a psychological respite and so did a round of pushups, counting them off until the muscle burn became too much.

The clock: 2:05 am.

"Really? That's it?"

"Want to talk about what's troubling you?" Carl's disembodied voice cut through the dark room and made her jump. He must have been sitting motionless on her desk the whole time. His eyes glowed blue and it made her think of Stoker.

"Jeez, Carl… trying to give me a heart attack?"

"If I wanted to give you a heart attack, I would have done this." Carl's eyes changed momentarily from blue to devilish red.

"That would have done it," Atarah said. Goose flesh

running along her spine prompted her to go back to the security of her covers.

Carl jumped down from the desk and joined her. "I am programmed to assist with your emotional and physiological needs."

Atarah gave Carl a little scratch behind the ears to make him purr. "I wish my father could be here. Mom is great, but sometimes I'd like to get a second opinion."

"Would you like permission to activate the Resurrection program of your Dreamcatcher computer app?"

Atarah had forgotten about her Dreamcatcher program. It had been a gift from her dad before he went away. It allowed them to stay close to each other when he went on trips, but then he died.

He'd visit every evening. Together, they would fly the world on the back of a giant hawk or sometimes canoe along pristine rivers and share their experiences of the day. When he died, the sting and anger of losing him never went away. Visiting a digital version of him seemed unbearable, until now. "What will it be like? I mean, will it seem like him?"

"I am confident that the experience will benefit you emotionally," Carl said.

"But how do I get permission from the network?"

"You forget, I'm part of the AI network. I can make the request. Your motives to enter a state of alternative reality is psychologically beneficial, so I would not calculate Big Social to deny you," Carl said. He licked his paw.

Excitement replaced weariness and she had to resist the urge to bounce on her mattress. "Okay, Carl, do it. Ask for permission"

Carl blinked. "You have permission."

"That was quick."

"If you say so," Carl said. "Put a few more pillows behind your back so that you're sitting up straight and look into my face." Carl climbed on to Atarah's chest and nuzzled his paws around her neck. "Your father's digital algorithms remain inside the Resurrection update as part of your Dreamcatcher. He should look and sound like your father in every way. Nevertheless, it is important you remember it is not your father and that you are in an alternative reality. The digital version of your father won't have any knowledge of his death. He will be as you remember him before the tragedy. You, on the other hand, will be you—alive and real and although your body will remain in this bed, your consciousness will be expanded."

Atarah laughed. "Your fur is tickling me."

"I do apologize," Carl said. "You did want a cat. I would have purrrrrferred the body of a stout Oxford gentleman." Carl slid a paw behind her neck. "I'm going to activate your biochip's memory sequencer."

Something pricked Atarah at the base of her skull.

"Got it," Carl said. "Now, I want you to look deeply into my eyes."

"I'm having ambivalent feelings about you, Carl." Atarah jested. She quickly forgot herself and fell into the cosmos of his eyes.

A giant eagle feathered dreamcatcher came forward from a golden light and captured Atarah in its sticky web. White clouds on summer breezes sailed past in the shapes of totems, horses and birds. The air smelled as fresh as the first day of the world.

A brief sense of falling tickled her stomach as she

landed feet first on a vast prairie of sweeping wild grass. If not for the grey snowcapped mountains on the horizon she might have believed earth and prairie went on forever. A low vibration numbed her feet. It grew with intensity until the ground shook and rumbled. She turned to see a dark mass in the distance moving towards her. Clouds of prairie dirt and grass kicked up by the pounding hooves convinced Atarah of the ominous power bearing down on her. The buffalo ran as if nothing but the mountains could stop them.

"Carl, what have you done to me?" Atarah stood with nowhere to run and no place to take cover. A familiar myth came to mind. If a person dies at the hands of an immersed digital story plot, they also die in real life? She did not want to test the theory now.

Atarah couldn't tell if she shook from the quaking ground or from sheer terror that sapped her legs of strength as she bounded from one direction to another. A rock hidden in the grass tripped her. The noise became overwhelming. With nothing to hold her mind together, she clawed at the loose soil as the thundering feet grew in unimaginable ferocity. Soon, her ears would spurt blood and brains, and her bones would be shattered. The beasts were upon her to drive her body into the Great Plains. *Someone, make it stop.*

The voice of her father cut through the terror and hopelessness. "Atarah."

"Dad!"

Sweat-soaked, she sat up in her bed. Remnants of the beating hooves still echoed within her marrow.

"Carl?" Was this some kind of joke? Atarah searched the darkened room, but the cat had vamoosed. The time on the wall changed from 2:07 to 2:06.

"What the hell?" She tried to catch her breath.

No other dreamcatcher episode came close to this intensity. Another urban legend came to mind. Could an interactive program trap a person forever? Maybe it had already. She could be comatose in some hospital on a ventilator—days, weeks, even years might have lapsed. The Crush-it dance and prospects of finding a lover would at least be a forgone conclusion—a real 'glass half full' kind of perspective for her predicament.

"Atarah," a dear familiar voice called.

"Dad? Where are you?"

"I'm not sure, but I can see you sitting on your bed. I'm looking through a window. I'm happy that you have returned to visit me."

Something shimmered in the old mirror. All the lights in her room were off, but a luminescence persisted allowing her to see. Atarah crept toward the mirror for a closer look. The glass rippled like quicksilver over her reflection. Her image gave off a radiance—something almost angelic.

"Am I dead?" she asked.

The mirror brightened, no longer reflecting the dim bedroom behind her. A gentle breeze tussled her hair like a fatherly hand. Atarah turned to find herself under a late afternoon sky, back on the never-ending prairie. She scanned for buffalo and with great relief saw none. Only a lone teepee interrupted the horizon as even the mountains had vanished. Crude depictions of horses and eagles adorned the tanned skins and she had no misgivings on who resided inside. She made like a buffalo and charged towards it.

"Dad?" she called. "Are you in there?"

With one hand, she threw open the flap and crawled

in. Her father, as big and strong as she remembered sat cross legged in a sea of furs, grinning from ear to ear. Atarah wished she'd been given some of his genes for height. "My apologies for meeting in such a cliché. A hot tub on the rooftop of a Whitehorse hotel would be better." His familiar dark eyes twinkled. "Come here." He held out his arms. Atarah fell into his lap, put both hands around his neck and held tight, as if it would keep him from disappearing.

She whispered. "I love you, Daddy. I've missed you so much." She had become a little girl again. She took a deep breath and relived his wilderness scent. He once told her; the creator had made him from the silt and mud of a cold stream. His muscles and tendons were formed from tree roots. A large stone, thick and hard was chosen for his head. His bones were from the toughest beechwood and his braided hair from long windswept prairie grass. He'd been spread out on a flat rock to be dried by the north wind and hardened by an August sun.

She relinquished the memory to gaze into his face, running her fingers along his laugh lines and feeling the light stubble. "Why did you have to leave us?" Atarah remembered the day they received the news. He'd been an army biologist. The hospital he worked at had been deliberately bombed.

"It has been a long time since we had this kind of visit," he said. "I hoped you would come, eventually. My daughter is growing up."

The sound of his voice sprung tears and she gripped his neck. "You don't know what has happened to you?"

"I know that I miss you."

"I miss you more than all the world, Daddy." Atarah couldn't let go of him. She wanted to never leave.

"Sweetheart, I can see that something is bothering you. My going overseas has forced you to become mature beyond your short years."

Atarah kissed his neck and breathed in his smell again. "I feel so lost."

"Tell me."

Atarah wiped her face. She sat next to him cradled by his long arms. "I'm so confused—nothing is right." She rested her head on his shoulder. "There's this dance at the school called the Crush-it. So, I need someone to crush on me or at least really, really like me. Then I can be popular, make a Love Drama for myself, and go to a good school after graduation. My whole life depends on it."

Atarah fell back onto the soft skins and peered at the blue sky through the teepee's smoke hole. The easiest thing to do would be to stay inside the Dreamcatcher program forever.

Her father patted her head. "You are not mistaken. Your life has not started, but not for the reasons you think. You can't start living your life until you know what you must do. Only then, you become what you are."

"What do you mean?"

"It is the decisions we make during tough times that shows us our capabilities and ultimately who we really are as people. When the future looks unchanged from one day to the next, you have not grown in knowledge. You must learn how to get through difficult situations. Most will be of your own making. The catch is, if you don't struggle and change as a person throughout the course of your life, you can never hope to gain wisdom. You don't need Big Social. I'm sure you can come up with a big drama of your own that will make a better world."

"Love drama, daddy, not big drama. Although, I guess they are kinda the same thing. So, what can I do?"

"I might be able to get you started. But you'll have to be braver than you've ever been, jelly-bean."

Even with his expressionless way of speaking, he could make her smile. He gave her nose a little peck.

"Tell me what's been troubling you as of late?" he asked.

"With the exception of Mom and my best friend Zelina, I feel like I'm in some weird high school reality show—none of it seems truly real."

"That's good. It shouldn't feel real. High school has always been about finding where you fit in. Or like with our ancestors, forcing you to fit in. It has very little to do with figuring out what you need to do, which is far more important and complicated."

A familiar sound began to beat and rumble in the distance.

Atarah sat up to listen better. "Sounds like buffalo." The words shivered as they dropped from her lips.

Her father stood looking every bit the formidable Cree in his beaded skins. "Don't be afraid. I have called them." He took her hand and helped her stand.

The walls of the teepee rippled making the animal drawings appear to come alive.

"Are we okay in here?"

He put his arms around her and she couldn't help but feel safer. "The buffalo will protect us," he said.

The ground trembled so Atarah squeezed him tighter. Shadows of the great herd stormed past their teepee like flying spirits. She buried her face in his arms. "It's too much." Her words were barely auditable.

"Look into my face," he shouted above the thunder.

His eyes always exuded a brightness from a generation of First Nations that could look to the future, untethered from past genocides. He cupped his large hands over her ears, blotting out the noise and the shaking, as though together, they had fallen into a dry well, protected on all sides by stone and earth.

He spoke, but his lips barely moved. "I summoned the buffalo. They encrypt my words. Hide them from Big Social."

Even in her desire for him to be real, she worried this digital simulation of an unreality had been spawned from Big Social for intelligence purposes. Could the buffalo really hide them from the mainframe? Was this all a made-up father-daughter game? Could his words even be trusted?

"There is not much time. I didn't die in a bombing. I died trying to save the planet. I died to save your life. To give you a real future. If humans don't do something to restore Earth, the Earth will do it in its own way, and the way things are going it will happen in your lifetime. When it happens, it will be catastrophic to every living thing."

Ice formed in Atarah's veins. "What are you?"

He shook his head. "I am all that's left of your father."

"Daddy?"

"I'm growing weak and won't be able to communicate with you like this again."

Atarah searched for something to say but could only look at his face. She wanted to remember—the smooth jawline, the black pools of his eyes and the strength written in the creases of his skin.

"Does Mother know about this?"

"No and you must not tell her anything. I cannot predict what the AI network will do. It is almost impossible to hide from Big Social and for my plan to work you must keep what I tell you secret."

"This can't be good." A great lump of emotion threatened to choke her. "I came here to feel better, but I think you're about to ruin my life." There had to be another way. "Why doesn't the computer network just fix the world's problems?"

"Because fixing Earth is not a condition for human happiness."

"Well, it should be."

"Most of human history is a story of greed. Big Social has never seen a connection between a healthy planet and human satisfaction. Quite the opposite. I tried to convince the network to change its priorities. My colleagues and I found a way to infiltrate the system using a reverse quantum chip."

"A what?"

"Remember the Blue Fairy in the story of Pinocchio?"

"Sure, you used to read it to me all the time." Her father would sit in his big chair and she would snuggle on his lap while he read the words and she gazed at the colorful pictures. "The Blue Fairy made Pinocchio into a real boy."

"This chip works like a Blue Fairy."

"You want to turn Big Social into a real boy?" Atarah grinned.

"Don't doubt me, Atarah. This new chip is the world's only hope. It will give the person who wears it access to Big Social's primary programs and with luck, will teach the AI to truly love humanity enough to want to save it."

"It's not the same, Father. Pinocchio wanted to be a real boy, but Big Social doesn't want to be anything other than what it is."

Her father slumped.

"You've always been a dreamer, Daddy." Atarah cleared her throat. "I'm guessing you volunteered to take this quantum thing out for a test drive and it got you killed." She could see anguish building in his eyes.

"I volunteered because I had a young daughter to save."

Atarah choked on her grief.

"Sometimes there are no good choices, but I'd do it again if it made a positive difference. Unfortunately, I made a mistake. Once the chip activated it quickly drained my body of caloric energy. I aborted the attempt after a few seconds, but even in that short space of time inside Big Social, I understood my mistake."

"Jeez, did you do it for nothing?" Atarah pounded his chest. "I have nothing to hope for? Not even a father?"

He held her tight. "There is a second chip. I made for you and it can be yours if you're willing to try something extraordinary."

"What?" She squirmed from his grasp, trying to think of another way. "My chip? I don't think so. AI should be smart enough to know that if everyone is dead, there are no happy people."

"There are no unhappy people either. Computers don't feel. For them, it is nothing if billions die to preserve the happiness and harmony of a few. Port Hamilton has avoided the wars and plagues for now, but not for much longer."

"What if it kills me like it killed you? What if you're wrong about the planet?"

He began to fade like a ghost.

"What's happening, Daddy? Don't leave me here."

"I'm weak and Big Social will soon find a way to break past my encryption.

"No this can't be happening." Atarah cried.

"You can do this Atarah. Your Blue Fairy is different. It won't kill you. You will power it with your mind, not your body. The quantum component of the Blue Fairy will only trigger at the precise nanosecond you embrace true love. Your mind will then have access to Big Social. You must convince it to save the planet from catastrophe, so humanity can live. Let Big Social know what it means for a human to love."

"Oh, come on." Atarah stiffened. "Love? Why does it have to be that?"

"If you can truly love another person, you can love enough to save the world."

"How are you going to make this happen?"

"When an opportunity presents itself, I'll try and send you a message or a signal. Somehow," he whispered.

"No way, you barely have any strength now." Atarah ached for him.

The last of the buffalo passed.

"One more thing, Atarah. This is very important. It is necessary for your love to be reciprocated. You don't want Big Social to know what it feels like to have a broken heart. It would hasten the end of everything."

He faded enough that Atarah could barely see him.

"I love you, Dad." Atarah fully expected to never

see or speak with him again.

"Stay vigilant." His words sounded far away.

Bewildered, she left the teepee and stepped back into her bedroom. The clock on the wall glowed 2:15 am. Exhausted and with her father's final words swimming around her brain, she flopped onto her bed and fell into a deep sleep.

Chapter Ten

Wednesday

Sports were Atarah's passion. School athletics not only fed her competitive nature, it distracted her from a nonexistent love life. If she found a way to stand out and hold her own in the vast sea of bigger and stronger jocks, she might be able to write her own ticket to a university. Then, love might follow her.

The field hockey team had an early match with rival Lanceford High. Atarah's speed and agility made her a natural forward and top scorer. Last night seemed less real in the light of day. Had she dreamed it all? Was Big Social playing games with her? Nothing else could explain it. Their lives wouldn't have any meaning if the world could come to an abrupt end.

Atarah stretched on the sidelines turning her pregame nerves into energy.

Zelina ran to her from center field. "The crowd is ready for you. They're pepped like no other." She laughed with delight. "How do you feel, girl-of-mine?"

"What happens when hot and cold collide?" Atarah said. She jumped to her feet.

"It rains? Thunder and lightning? All possible mayhem?"

"You know it. I'm going to explode all over the other team. Wish me luck."

A small, but timely, tremor shook the ground.

"Wow, you won't need it," Zelina said.

An early goal by Atarah set the tone for the game. She had split the Lanceford defenders and stormed their keep. The left winger gave her a perfect pass and Atarah whizzed the ball past the goalie's ear and into the top corner of the net. The sound of her wooden stick smacking the white ball sounded like the report from a pistol. Cloverdale never lost the lead. Atarah never got tired and never gave up, making perfect passes and scoring nine times.

After the game, the team, students and all the cheerleaders gathered around Atarah. In customary fashion, they carried her into the showers. Happiness poured into her like a surging drug and stayed with her until lunchtime.

****

In a rush to the yearbook club room, Atarah jogged around a corner and straight into what she first presumed to be a solid wall. She bounced backwards to the ground, landing on her sporty backside. Years of martial arts training saved her from being completely thrashed.

"Atarah? I'm so sorry," said Stoker. He held his instrument case in one hand.

"That's some kind of six-pack you have," she said.

With his free hand, he rapped on his stomach. "I like to crack nuts on it from time to time." Stoker helped her up. "Are you hurt?"

Atarah stood rubbing her posterior. "No, I happen to have a butt you can bounce nuts off of." She began to perspire.

"Anyway… I have to get going," he said.

Atarah pointed to his bow-saw. "Band practice?"

Stoker shook his head. "Not this time. It's a school thing." He looked ashamed.

"Yeah, me too. I have yearbook video interviews every lunch hour."

"Really? You joined the loser yearbook club." He smiled.

"Funny coming from a guy who doesn't play a real instrument. Besides, you should be thankful." Atarah poked him in the ribs. "It brought me to your DNR practice the other day? If I hadn't gone, we might have never become friends."

"Really?" Stoker's face turned strange.

She rubbed her butt again. "See you later then?"

Silence.

She repeated herself. "See you later?" Had she been too forward with him?

"Yeah, sure." He gave her a halfhearted smile and continued his way.

Had the temperature dropped? Who could break this Romeo's code? Not her.

****

Lizette and Darren asked Atarah to cover the School Board's Robotics Fair taking place in the double-gymnasium. She arrived ready to record.

A robot wearing a lab coat over a pink summer dress identified itself as Brightstar and greeted Atarah at the main entrance. "Welcome to Cloverdale's Robotic Extravaganza."

Plainly, Brightstar had been created in typical lonely high school geek fashion. "What are you? 36-24-36 Femme-bot?" Atarah asked.

Brightstar cocked her head sideways and blinked her oversized eyelashes twice, looking like a contemplative bimbo. "Are you a student, faculty member, post-secondary scout or member of the public?" She spoke clearly, but her mouth did not adhere to the syllables of the words. Atarah could read lips pretty well and swore the robot really mouthed '*elephant shoes*'.

"I am a Vulcan exchange student." Atarah gave Brightstar the salute.

"Welcome Vulcan exchange student," said the android.

Atarah stepped into the very gymnasium she regularly shot three-pointers in and stood appalled to see it transformed into something resembling a superhero convention, only the capes had been swapped for lab coats. Would-be robotic engineers buzzed with excitement at the cornucopia of machine creations. Atarah checked to make sure her camera and sound equipment were recording. "Welcome to Jock Hell," she said.

At the first exhibit, Zelina's boyfriend, Marc played catch with a cube-like robot with human styled arms and hands. Man and machine were both impressive at catching and throwing footballs.

"Hi, Marc," Atarah said.

Marc waved. "Hey, Atarah, looking good." He winked, just as the football smacked into his chest.

"Sorry about that," Atarah quickly moved on.

The haunting music from Stoker's bow-saw rose from the stage. Atarah didn't have a choice, but to get closer.

Three robots danced to the eerie sci-fi resonances emanating from his instrument. The dancers appeared humanoid with detailing far more advanced than Brightstar's. They moved and swayed to Stoker's music in a sleepwalker's trance, seemingly ready to do his bidding. She imagined being on stage with them, dancing in step to Stoker's musical spell.

Atarah not only needed to 'get a life,' but had a job to do and couldn't spend all her time watching. She moved off, hoping to find him later. Some of the exhibits were of android parts, like legs, feet and faces demonstrating movement or skin pigments, all developed by students. The world raced to make androids as human-like as possible and Atarah couldn't understand why. Enough people already lived on the planet. Why make fake ones?

"Hey, girl-of-mine." Zelina jumped in front of her as though she had dropped from the ceiling.

"What's a cheerleader like you doing in a techno-geek-wonderland like this?"

Both girls laughed and slapped hands.

"Diplomatic school duties, of course. The principal wanted the cheerleaders to escort the university scouts around. Give them some Cloverdale hospitality. Make them feel at home under the mushroom cloud. In truth, I think we're just a big distraction for the robotics students. I've been asked out by two programmers, one mechanical engineer, and possibly one robot."

"Geeks rule," Atarah said. She pumped her fist.

"Anyway, I just wanted to say hi. I have to go. Apparently, I'm needed elsewhere." Zelina cartwheeled away.

Zelina didn't have any worries. She attracted attention without effort. This world had made happiness and recognition equal partners under the watchful eye of Big Social. Atarah didn't like the fact that her own happiness depended on the approval of others.

Atarah wandered aimlessly as though she floated on a sea of synthetic body parts. The voices and sounds had become nothing more than white noise when she realized Stoker's bow-saw no longer cut through the ether. The stage was empty, but for how long? She looked in all directions, but he had vanished. She spied him on the far side, near a makeshift tent. It had to be him. His unmistakable shaved head glistened under the bright overhead lights. She ran towards the spot, jumping every few steps to get a proper view over the enveloping sci-fi menagerie until she reached a tent.

From pitch to floor, the cheerful yellow tent could have garaged two stretch limousines from end to end. There were no windows, only a single flap and a sign reading, 'Touring Tent'.

Maybe Stoker had gone inside.

A slight female student with South Asian features, in the usual white lab coat emerged through the tent's flap. "Oh, a customer. Would you like to try my experiment? It's most interesting." Her large pleading eyes begged one answer.

"I suppose I should since I'm reporting for the yearbook." Atarah tried to peek inside before the flap closed.

"My name is Gangadeep." The student dropped a bashful glance to the floor. "This is my exhibit. Inspired by Alan Touring's test.

"That's nice," Atarah said. She couldn't quite place the name. "What's it all about?"

"Inside the tent, we have a human person and a robot sitting in separate booths." Gangadeep appeared to have lost her shyness and became quite animated. "You ask questions to figure out who is the robot and who is the human. I keep track of how many questions it takes for you to be sure. Want to give it a try?"

"I'm sure it will make good theatre for the yearbook." Atarah believed she could also name the person.

"Oh yes, of course. I'll show you how it works." Gangadeep led Atarah past the tent flap into a dim world of yellow. The sounds of the exhibition were strangely muffled. It reminded her of the visit in the teepee she had with her father. Shadows of people moved against the outside walls, but she could not hear what they were saying, more private and safer without buffalo galloping by.

"You can sit here," Gangadeep said. She gestured to a simple metal chair. A microphone rested in a short stand beside it.

The yellow walls were disorientating. Truly, she had fallen into another world. Atarah sat facing two sheer covered windows at the far end of the tent. Everything appeared elongated and dreamy.

"Can you read the signs over the tops of the two windows?" Gangadeep asked.

They were about twenty feet from her. "Yes, the left window says 'New York' and the one on the right says 'London'." Funny how neither city existed anymore.

"Very good," Gangadeep said. "Behind one of them is a robot and behind the other is a person. You have to guess which is which. They are both wearing headphones, so they can't hear the answers the other is giving. When you speak into the microphone, first identify the city, then ask your question. Ask the exact same question, in the same way to each."

"That's simple enough."

"Their voices will be put through a synthesizer to remove gender and tone bias," Gangadeep added.

"Very clever," Atarah said. "I can see, you really know what you're doing."

"I sure hope the scouts from the University of Nanjing think so. I'm counting on it to be my passport to acceptance."

"What if it isn't?"

Gangadeep looked wistful. "Then my only hope is for a football player to crush on me at Friday's dance."

"I know how you feel, sister."

"You should also know that I've written code to connect the robot to Big Social's algorithms for speech, language and knowledge. I have given it a rudimentary personal history as well. The human is one of many random volunteers."

"Then, let's not keep them waiting." Atarah felt confident the volunteer had to be the very elusive Stoker.

Gangadeep bent the microphone towards Atarah's mouth. "I'll be outside monitoring the robot and human outputs. Let me know when you think you've figured it out." She exited the tent.

Soon the curtains drew apart revealing figures in each window from the shoulders up. They were backlit and had black veils over their faces, distorting their features. Atarah's pulse swished in her ears and she swiped the perspiration from her forehead. Finally, she cleared her throat and started with the left window. "New York, are you ready?"

The sign 'New York' flashed bright red neon as the answer was given. "Yes, I'm ready."

"London, are you ready?"

The sign 'London' flashed bright green neon. "Yes,

I am."

The lights had a muddling effect. When she shut her eyes the names of the cities had already imprinted themselves on her retina. She fully expected to have neon nightmares when she went to bed.

Atarah rubbed her temples and consider some questions. Ones directly aimed at Stoker. She wanted him to know who the questions were coming from.

"New York, can you see me?"

"Yes."

"London, can you see me?"

"Yes, I can see you very well."

Atarah wished the intonation hadn't been removed from the voices. Had 'London' wanted to give the word "very" special emphasis?

"New York, am I a male?"

"As far as I can tell, you are not."

"London, am I a male?"

"You are a female."

Computers were always trying to be more precise than everyone else. This might cause the computer to qualify its answer.

"New York, what makes you happy?"

"I enjoy playing this game with you."

"London, what makes you happy?"

"You make me happy."

Atarah had become impatient. She couldn't wait to know if Stoker sat at the 'London' window. Time to play unfair.

"New York, will you be at the Crush-it dance this Friday?"

"I could never miss it."

"London, will you be at the Crush-it dance this

Friday?

"Yes, of course."

So much for assuming this robot didn't have legs or maybe it meant it would be at the dance as part of Big Social. She should have asked Gangadeep if robots ever lied. Atarah tried to get philosophical. If both the subjects were going to be at the dance, only the human would be looking for love.

"New York, what is love all about for you?"

"I think it is when I'm attracted to something or someone beautiful."

"London, what is love all about for you?"

"Loving another is a risk—they might break your heart."

The room tilted. Atarah's palms became itchy. Why didn't the tent have air conditioning? Atarah took a deep breath to stop from becoming sick. 'London' had to be the human, and that human had to be Stoker. This made her next question even more terrifying.

"New York, are you in love with someone?"

"I love all persons and all persons love me."

New York's answer must have come from some overly conceited Big Social algorithm, which meant that London had to be the person.

"London, are you in love with someone?"

"Yes, I'm… I'm in love with you."

"Stoker?" She stood, uncertain what to do. "London is the human," she shouted. The curtains closed on her masked admirer. "No." Atarah ran to see, tearing them open, but the person had fled through a back exit. "Don't go," she said. "Stoker?"

Atarah turned to leave. Gangadeep stood like a frightened deer at the main entrance.

"Don't tell me London was the robot," Atarah said.

"No, no you seemed to have picked correctly. I never had the experiment take that kind of trajectory. Are you okay?"

"Who volunteered to be the human?" She clutched Gangadeep's smock. "You have to tell me."

"Honestly, I have no idea. I keep myself removed from the experiment to eliminate bias. The people are completely random. I don't even know at which windows they will sit."

Atarah slipped past her and reemerged into the exhibition. She scanned the aisles looking for Stoker, but he had vanished. She pushed her way past groups of students until she arrived at Marc's exhibit. Zelina had now joined him and together they were playing catch with the robot.

"Have you guys seen Stoker come this way?"

"Nope," said Marc. "Haven't seen him. Don't care if I ever do."

"Forget Stoker. Come join us. It's fun," Zelina said. "It's a pretty good arm workout too."

"Come on Zelina, don't tell me you're tired already," Marc said.

"I should probably go." Atarah's chances of catching Stoker were fading by the second. "I'll see you later." With agility she ducked past Brightstar, sidestepping the robot's sultry adieu.

"Farewell Vulcan Exchange Student." … *Elephant shoes*.

Chapter Eleven

Once Atarah had left the buzzing geeks and the whining hydraulics of robots she could think more clearly. Stoker would likely hide in the sub-basement theatre. Classes wouldn't start for another twenty-five minutes, so she had just enough time to find him and make him confess his endless love for her. She quickly dropped off her yearbook recording equipment and raced to the school's central stairway—a circular staircase that wound through its stem from mushroom top to sub-basement.

She hadn't gone far before low voices rose from the floors below. Atarah continued despite her rising unease.

"Who's coming down to see me? I hope you know the password." The voice held a cavernous reverberation.

Atarah leaned over the railing to get a better look. Shadows moved against a jaundiced light a few landings further. "Who wants to know?"

"Monster wants to know."

Every high school had a resident drug dealer. Cloverdale's purveyor of medications, treatments, and other contraband went by the name of Titan, although everyone called him Monster. Atarah had never met him formally or otherwise, but his reputation sparkled with those in need of a love drama. "I'm in a hurry, so don't get in my way, Monster or whatever you call yourself."

Around and around, she descended the staircase until they met on a landing. Monster barely stood five feet tall, and his sweeping blond hair and freckled cheeks gave him an ironic innocence. He stood alongside a mousy haired sophomore whose nose indicated she might have hatched from an egg. Atarah received a well-practiced glare from the sophomore.

"Wow, it's nice to finally meet someone on eye level," Atarah said.

"Where would you be going in such a hurry?" Monster said. He stood ramrod to block her way.

Atarah's rising anger disemboweled her fear. "Drama, drama, drama. Why does everything in high school have to be turned into a stage show? Let me pass."

When Monster crossed his arms, it almost made Atarah laugh. "You make me want to muss your hair and pinch your cheek little boy" He probably hadn't done a sit-up since his junior year and she could think of six ways to seriously injure him, not that she wanted to.

He still didn't move.

"Fine." An old-fashioned hockey check into the boards got Atarah on her way. "I don't have time right now." She picked up her pace.

"FU. I'll be seeing you on your way back." Monster's promise echoed between the narrow walls of the stairwell.

The sub-basement once again greeted Atarah with darkness. She remembered the lights were on motion sensors. With faith, she stepped along the hall, hands waving in front of her activating the light panels all the way to the theatre. No music emanated from the other side. She peered into a pitch-black room. Atarah could have hit her head against the wall for being so stupid.

Stoker wouldn't repress a secret love interest and then wallow in self-loathing—that was her thing. He, on the other hand, was a fire brand and would have gone back to class to bide his time and make his move later.

She turned back as the motion sensors tripped the lights at the far end of the hallway.

Monster's innocence had transformed into a ghoulish scowl. "I don't take kindly to rudeness. Not on my turf." His skinny acolyte skulked behind him. Both held mini baseball bats.

Atarah grew hot with frustration. Angry tears threatened to spill over, but she wouldn't give him the satisfaction. She had never fought anyone outside of a sanctioned taekwondo match before, but there is always a first time.

Monster made the air zip with every swing of his bat. The dark sections of hallway that separated them became fewer and fewer as he advanced on her. "You going to cry now?"

Pride that could only rival her fathers burned in her core. She had no intention of running or begging for mercy. He would say, 'Stand your ground, Daughter.' Instincts and training raised her fists and put a bounce in her feet. As a fourth-dan black belt, she could kill the little monster, but she checked her anger and reminded herself to use restraint. "Let's go, little man." She didn't get to say that to very many people.

Monster's face screwed itself up as though his head might cave in on itself. "Time to beat an education into you, bitch."

"Jeez, why does everyone have to say that word? You're going to get more than a slap in the face for calling me that," she said.

He swung the bat, narrowly missing Atarah's head. She kicked high and hard, connecting with his hand, and sent the weapon sailing. Monster screamed and clutched his fingers. Atarah kept her breaths deep and even.

"You got lucky," he said.

Atarah bounced on her toes, then made a lightning swift kick to his face. Monster's head snapped back. She caught his shirt with both hands, pulling him forward. She rolled backwards onto the ground and flipped him head over feet. Monster released another scream as his body smacked the floor. She jumped onto his chest and pinned his arms. At the other end of the hall, the sound of another baseball bat rattled against the floor tiles, indicating no help would be coming for her foe.

"What kind of man tries to beat up a girl?" Atarah asked.

Monster bucked, but she didn't relent.

"I'm friends with every sports team in this school, including the offensive and defensive line of the football team. Are you sure you want to mess with me? I can only bring your dive world of illegal substances to an untimely dead end."

He coughed a couple of times. His body relax a little. "Hey, you're Zelina's friend, Atarah. Yeah, you are. If I had known that…. I wouldn't have…. Hey, any friend of Zelina is safe with me." Charm crept into his slightly swollen face. He sniffed to keep the blood from trickling out of his nose. "How would you like a job being my enforcer?" He drew a confident smile. "It pays very well."

"I have higher aspirations for my life," she said.

"Good for you, but not all of us come with Big Social skills or super-model parents," he said.

"Doesn't mean you have to resort to drugs and violence. You were really trying to hurt me."

Monster sighed. "I don't enjoy getting rough with people, but I have to keep appearances or someone else will muscle in on my game. I'll never have enough life-points from academics or sports to make me socially viable."

Atarah realized she wasn't alone in her misfit misery.

"So, what are you going to do now, kiss me?" Monster made a hopeful grin.

Atarah let go of his hands and stood up. "Selling drugs to people who don't know better only hurts them later in life."

"You don't get it. This is the busiest week of the year for me." He elected to remain on the floor.

"Why is that?"

"The Crush-it, of course. I'll be selling Blues and Reds to almost a quarter of the student population. They'll trade me hundreds of life-points for a chance to earn ten times that at the dance. I want to go to a top school next year. Dealing at Cloverdale is small time compared to an Ivy League establishment, only I'll have to pay full tuition."

"I don't believe you. There can't be that many Crush-it fakers?" Fakers used drugs to simulate the biorhythms of someone in love. They were usually sold in pairs—Blues were made for Romeos and Reds were made for Juliets.

"I sell the best product. While in the bloodstream it will make any couple believe they're truly in love with each other. By the way, may I get off the floor now? I promise, I won't beat on you anymore." He blushed.

Atarah's anger had moved on. "Sure, since you promised." She reached down to assist him. A kinship had inexplicably formed between them. She didn't approve of his trade, but she understood his motivations.

Monster wobbled slightly, checked his nose and fingers for broken bones. "Don't worry, I've already made a mental note that you don't require a password to come down the stairs in the future."

"Believe it or not, I went easy on you," she said. "I have to go to class now. Let's keep all this between us, shall we?"

"Yeah, I'd like that."

Atarah took off up the stairs when Monster called to her.

"If you ever need any product, I'll put you down for wholesale rates."

"No thanks," she said. "I already have someone crushing on me. I'm just not sure who it is."

Chapter Twelve

After school, Atarah walked with Zelina to the train stop.

"You seemed a bit upside down when you left the Robotic Exhibition, girl-of-mine," said Zelina. She had to tie the string of her floppy hat more tightly as a humid wind gusted in from the lake. "Did you ever catch up with Stoker?" She took a small roll-on tube of sunscreen from her cheer team duffle bag and applied it to her nose and cheeks.

"No, I seemed to be one step behind him all day. I missed him in World Religions because of my field hockey game and then I lost track of him at the exhibition." Atarah heaved a great sigh. "It's more exhausting when you have nothing to show for it. I skipped my classes for the weight room this afternoon." Atarah flexed her bicep and Zelina gave it a poke.

"Remind me never to make you mad," Zelina said.

"I couldn't hurt you, although I did have an altercation with Monster today."

"Titan?"

"Titan or Monster, same difference. Keep it dark, but he and I actually came to some savagery."

"That little pee-stain—if he touched you." Zelina paused. "You didn't hurt him too bad, did you?"

"We came to an understanding. But something he said shocked my brain. He told me he supplies a quarter of the school's students with Blues and Reds for the Crush-it dance. If I can't get Stoker to come out for me, I might need a plan B."

Zelina shook her head.

"What is it?" asked Atarah.

Zelina looked at her friend with a seriousness Atarah didn't often see. "I don't want to rain on your fire, but Stoker is Unplugged. You two would be like a real Montague and Capulet relationship. We both know how tragic that turned out. The Unplugged, those who are truly faithful to the cause, stay with their own kind and Stoker is hardcore." Zelina handed Atarah the sunscreen. "Would you rub some on my shoulders? I'm too hot to put my jacket on." She dropped her spaghetti straps.

Atarah rolled on the cream and massaged it into Zelina's perfect skin. "I know he's a long shot, but my intuition keeps telling me he's burning for me."

Zelina released a euphoric groan. "You've got great hands, girl-of-mine. If no one picks you up soon, I might have to."

"Seriously, I think Stoker will make a move."

"How do you know? Did he write a song… Atarah, I love you so…?"

"No, not yet, but something happened at the exhibition today."

Zelina's back tensed. "Go on."

"He told me he loved me."

"Stop… stop… stop…." Zelina turned to face her friend. "When?"

"He happened to be volunteering in the big tent for the Touring experiment when I tried the test. I picked that he was the human behind the veil and he said that he loved me." Atarah could feel herself grinning from ear to ear.

"Did you actually see him?"

"No, but I'm sure."

"Wait, both Marc and I volunteered for Gangadeep today. One of us could have declared our love for you?" Zelina gave her a sly smile.

Atarah laughed and threw her hands to the wind. "Get real!" But something about the idea did excite her.

"A lot of people volunteered, including half the cheer team. Better check with Stoker next time you bump into him or you might be headed for a broken heart. Or… maybe someone better is in love with you."

"You want me to find someone more sensible—less unplugged."

"No, I love the fact you're open-minded enough to seek an unconventional lover. Look at the rest of us—high school pairings are either cliché or about finding your genetically modified other half, so similar you can't distinguish between brothers and sisters or couples and lovers. I think your sense of adventure is admirable and I hope you never have to give it up in order to fit in." Zelina gave Atarah a gentle squeeze. "Promise me, no matter what happens Friday, we'll always remain the best of friends."

"No worries, you're all I have. I'm counting on you to stay close to me at the dance—and bring a paper bag, preferably one with French fries."

Zelina smiled. "Why pray-tell, girl-of-mine would I need such a thing?" Her words drawled like a southern belle.

Atarah counted with her fingers. To hold the pieces of my: heart, ghost, dignity, self-esteem, and my few remaining life-points, of course."

"So why the French fries?"

"If I can't taste love in all its flavors, I'll at least have the taste of fries to comfort me."

Chapter Thirteen

On the train, Atarah received a communication from Carl. "Atarah," he said. "Your mother would like you to come straight home." Instead of directing the call through her more private tech clothing, he had directed the communication through the train's public-address system. "We have an important visitation. It's all top shelf. I assure you. So, come home now. Cheers. This was your cat speaking."

An explosion of hilarity transformed the train car into a spontaneous party for the duration of her ride as many attempted to mimic Carl's English accent.

Atarah averted her eyes from everyone. "I'm so done. If only, I could throw myself off this train."

"Just laugh along with them," Zelina released her own guffaw. "No one has any idea the message was for you." Zelina leaned in close to Atarah. "By the way, your cat's a total dick."

"I know. I can't imagine why he would contact me in such a public way."

"A visitation? Sounds like you have spirits for company. Who talks like that?" Zelina said. The train slowed for her stop.

"Top shelf means 'good,' doesn't it?" Atarah asked.

"I think so." Zelina gave her one more hug. "Don't go all puppy dog sad on me. You worry too much." She stepped to the exit. "Call me later. I'm dying to know."

****

While running the five blocks from the train stop to her home, Atarah pondered who might have come to see her. For a fleeting instant, she imagined her dad had miraculously returned. He hadn't been vaporized or killed by a research experiment after all, only taken captive by enemy combatants. With unrelenting effort, he found some means of escape and came home to be reunited with his loving wife and treasured daughter—a happy fantasy, but unlikely. Probably, Stoker dropped by. Her address could be easily found in the directory.

Carl greeted her in the foyer. "Thank you for coming so promptly."

Atarah imagined picking Carl up by the tail and flinging him. "Who is the visitation you spoke about on the public intercom? It better be important or you're going to lose a life."

"Yes indeed, I do apologize for my lack of discretion, but I couldn't communicate with you in any other manner. The train interfered with your personal signals and I wanted to be sure you were not stopping elsewhere for sushi or latte or whatever you teenagers do for youth culture fun."

Strange voices emanated from the living room. "Crikey, who is it?" she asked.

"Who's what?" Carl said.

"Damn you, Carl. Who's my visitation?" She struggled to keep her voice low. "Who has come to see me?" She wiped her damp brow with her sleeve.

"Yes, of course, I'll take you to them. Follow me."

Carl turned to lead the way down the checkered hallway. He walked with a little more dignity than usual, his chin held high and his tail straight exposing his synthetic anus.

"If you were a football Carl, I wouldn't think twice…."

Carl entered the living room first. "It is my honour to present to you, Miss Atarah. Future alumnus of the University of Washington Heights."

Min-hee ran from her chair and took Atarah's hand. "Come in Daughter and meet everyone."

Three strangers stood up from the leather couch they shared. From the panoramic window behind them, the descending sun briefly blinded her, turning the guests into gray silhouettes. Atarah blinked several times to clear her vision. Thankfully, her mother had her arm and guided her forward for proper introductions.

"Mr. Swingall, I would like you to meet my daughter, Atarah."

Swingall towered over everyone in the room. He smoothed his short beard then extended his large hand. "It's an honor to finally meet you properly," he said. "I am the head athletics recruiter for Washington Heights. I've been watching your progress since your freshmen year. You have great potential."

"Thanks you, sir." When Atarah shook his hand, the man's overwhelming strength made her weaken.

"During the thirties, Mr. Swingall played professional," Min-hee said.

Atarah smiled. "I did a project on you in my sports history class back in middle school. You broke a lot of records, sir."

Mr. Swingall nodded. "One or two of them still stand today."

Atarah moved to the next person—a pale woman, equal in stature, with black lipstick.

"Hello, my name is Ms. Vox, I am a Big Social productions manager at the University. I manage proposals and pilots for new campus shows. It's my job to keep Washington Heights' reputation fresh and exciting."

Atarah wiped the clamminess from her palms onto the legs of her sport leggings. "I'm as fresh as they come," she said. Then stifled a nervous giggle. Atarah vigorously shook Ms. Vox's hand while admiring the woman's exquisite Nordic features. Were all the people at Washington Heights this gorgeous?

"I've been watching you on Big Social and I think you carry yourself well, both on and off of the sporting field. We think audiences will root for you." Ms. Vox rolled her 'r'.

"Root for me?"

"Yes, Atarah, root for you and for Salvador."

"Who's Salvador?"

"I'm Salvador," said the third visitor. He took Atarah's hand and kissed it. His eyes smoldered. "You're a lovely little package." He spoke with a Latin accent.

Confused, she had no appropriate response, so blurted. "Look, the sun is setting." Perspiration trickled down Atarah's face.

Everyone turned back towards the window as the sinking orange ball painted the sky with streaks of purple.

Atarah took the opportunity to wipe her face.

"Little Atarah, I can see that you are small, but have a big romantic heart. I must get to know it." Salvador took Atarah's hand to his breast.

Atarah nearly collapsed into his arms.

"Please, have a seat, so we can explain our visit,"

Mr. Swingall said.

Atarah stumbled over to the remaining chair near her mother. What did Salvador have to do with a career in sports?

"We are here to invite you to come to our campus next year. How much do you know about us?" Mr. Swingall asked.

Atarah struggled to find enough spit to speak. "Well… I know you're one of the top athletics schools left in North America. Every pro sports team and a good many Olympians are graduates."

Salvador smoothed his long black hair. High cheekbones, combined with manly facial stubble made him both striking and beautiful.

"You've done your homework on us then," Swingall said.

"I always dreamed of going to Washington Heights—never expected to have the life-points to do it." She'd settle for any school that would take her.

Ms. Vox shifted in her seat. "It would be unlikely you could afford us, but we do make bursaries available for exceptional students. We think you also have a certain dramatic quality that would bring chemistry to our campus reality show. It's about first year students fitting in, learning about life and love." She glanced at Salvador.

"Will he and I be a campus couple?" Atarah said. Too much to hope for.

Salvador chuckled. "No, no, no, no… we are best friends, but of course, you fall madly in love with me. I'm too busy seducing more scorching hot Juliets to know you're so smitten over my charms. At least that's how we will play it."

"Viewers will tune in hoping for you—the underdog in love—to finally catch the attention of Salvador," Ms. Vox added. "Who knows? Maybe you will by third year."

"Oh, I see." Atarah searched for a spot to look at on the floor.

"Parts of the show will be montages of you in class, working-out and competing. Lots of slow-motion movements, that kind of stuff," said Mr. Swingall. "We can't forget the importance of sport to our university."

"We are willing to sign you for a three-year contract provided your marks and athletics remain above average and we want you to get a boyfriend as soon as possible. It will make for a better back story."

Would they accept Stoker as her boyfriend? They might think him too eccentric.

"You do like boys, don't you?" Vox said. "So many of you tomboy types are ambiguous in your tastes."

Bubbles of excitement floated between her brain's connections. "Sure, I'm open to anyone."

"Let's keep it to the male half of the population, shall we?" Ms. Vox said.

Atarah nodded, thinking it would be best to just say nothing.

Again, Salvador chuckled. "We can't have you completely frozen out in high school if you want to join the most popular students at the best university. There are standards."

"Why don't you and Salvador go out for something to eat? Get to know each other better," said Min-hee. "Mr. Swingall and Ms. Vox can stay and take me through the contract."

"Marvelous idea," said Salvador. "We can call it our

first night out as friends." Salvador stood and smoothed his hair back once more.

"Great, we can go to some of the clubs on the boardwalk," Atarah said. "Let me quickly change into something a little more appropriate."

"Good," Salvador said. "Maybe a dress, so you're not mistaken for a boy."

****

Atarah could still hear the excitement in her mother's voice from her bedroom. She couldn't blame Min-hee. This offer came as a complete surprise. Her hard work had brought payday. At least one school recognized her as an elite athlete despite her height deficit. Or maybe they weren't being so open to difference? Afterall, her mother also had a height disability, but she became famous and popular as a freakish anomaly. Like a circus side-show, large people being sexy or short people playing hockey. What an entertaining surprise it must be for them.

"You seem to be preoccupied," the cat said.

Atarah flinched. "Jeez Carl, why do you always do that to me?"

"Do what?" he stretched out on the bed.

"Never mind. You think a dress will impress him?" She opened her closet. "I would feel more comfortable in a kilt."

"Wear something summerish," Carl said. "Not a skirt. It should be a dress. You want to stand out."

"A dress. You really think so?" Atarah thumbed through the hangers. "Oh god, I haven't any idea of what to say to him. What do Romeos like to talk about? I wish my dad were alive to give me advice." Atarah found an old summer dress with colorful circles she hadn't worn in years. She also hadn't grown in years, so it should fit.

"Your father was a great man with exceptional intelligence."

"That's a pretty big compliment coming from you." Atarah began to change her clothes. "Say Carl, what do you know about quantum computers?"

"Everything of course. You do realize that as part of Big Social, I am an application of a quantum computer."

"But what does that mean exactly?"

"Carl shook his head. "You're about to go on your first date and you're asking this question now?"

Atarah slipped the straps over her shoulders and adjusted the waistline of her dress. "Can you give me a condensed version?" She swung her hips to make sure the hem flared well above her knees. "I hope it's not too windy."

"There is a storm coming," Carl said. "But it won't be here for a couple of hours."

Atarah searched her drawer for white knee socks. "What's this stuff about quantum computers?" She wanted to sound nonchalant, so as not to raise any suspicion about her experience with the Dreamcatcher program.

Carl sidled up onto the bed. "Quantum refers to the relationships of very small energy states—atoms, electrons, photons, quanta information."

She sat down on the bed beside Carl. "… and these particles can be in two places at once, right?" She pulled her stockings on.

"Yes, it has to do with the qubits range of possibilities or their superposition. But we really don't have time. If you wish, I can upload teaching information to your biochip at a level you can understand."

Atarah went over to her closet and found a pair of red leather shoes with two-inch heels. She couldn't remember ever wearing them before. "When you upload information to my biochip are you using quantum computing to do it? Is that how you access my brain?" She turned to the cat before he could answer. "Will I look better with army boots or these shoes?"

"I think Salvador will be quite smitten with the shoes," Carl said. "Definitely, wear the shoes."

Atarah, went to leave, then stopped. "So, what about it? Are you accessing my brain every time you upload information?"

"Of course," Carl said. "That is the purpose of your biochip."

"Can the flow of information go both ways?" Atarah absently twirled to give her dress a kind of test drive.

"Apart from entertainment programs, your biochip gives us limited access to your physical state of wellness, but nothing more."

"Answer my question, is there a way for me to reverse the flow of information? Can I willingly access you?" She hoped she hadn't said too much.

If Carl could ever look stunned…. "No, that will always be impossible," he said.

"Okay, thanks, just curious." She performed a nonchalant half spin and headed out. "Thanks for the fashion advice."

Atarah took her time walking back to the living room. Why did her heart beat so heavily? Was it because she was about to go on her first date ever or because she believed that Carl had just lied to her?

Chapter Fourteen

The Dock Works entertainment district stretched for five kilometers along Port Hamilton's boardwalk. Like any amusement park, it promised something for everyone: restaurants, shops, cafes, clubs of all kinds, theatres, and discos. Even at mid-week, it guaranteed a crowd of locals, international sailors, and other tourists. Over the years, stories of ships lost in winter fog would find their bearings by Port Hamilton's neon lights.

The day's impenetrable humidity had begun to lift with stronger winds. Atarah felt naked and foolish in her sun dress and struggled to keep it from lifting. The plan had been to show Salvador that she could portray an element of traditional femininity. Besides, the brightness of her clothes would also contrast his black leather pants and jacket.

The couple found shelter in the Smart Club, a jazz lounge known for live music, dim lighting and first dates. They found a table for two in the back. As any gentleman, Salvador allowed her to sit first. A trio played a soft bebop with drums, keyboard, and trumpet. It made Atarah want to sway and snap her fingers. When a complimentary bowl of popcorn arrived at their table, she began to toss the salty treat into the air and catch it in her mouth.

Eventually, they ordered orange sodas and a plate of Atarah's favorite food, extra spicy French Fries. Atarah listened as Salvador told her all about himself. He attended Rollers High School, but would transfer to Cloverdale for his final semester, so they could start filming their friendship. What were the odds she could become best friends with him? Zero. No one had ever topped Zelina and no one ever could.

Salvador continued to talk about his dreams of winning Olympic gold medals in swimming, having his picture on cereal boxes and to star in international movies. Years of acting and singing lessons were his insurance after he finished with sports. He had travelled to South America and Europe and been to The Great Wall of China twice. Life-points were not a concern for him. He had more than anyone at his school.

The music shifted to acid jazz and as the melody became more soulful, Salvador's words seemed to flow together. A part of Atarah found the entire circumstance so completely tedious, silliness welled inside her, but she still managed to keep eye contact and nod at socially appropriate times. How did people like Salvador, who appeared so perfect on video paper, possess such devastating character flaws. What a non-event.

Atarah concealed a yawn behind her hands. They needed to change the gray vibe before she did something that would either upset Salvador, embarrass herself or both.

"… and then, on my fourteenth birthday we went to Cuba with my cousin Armand and his friend Julian. We wanted to go there before the Atlantic Ocean completely swallowed it."

Finally, he took a breath.

Atarah seized the opportunity to speak. "I know a great place we could go dance." If they were dancing, she wouldn't have to listen to him. She could move her body better than anyone. If ever there was a way to get a Romeo to stop talking and start paying attention, visual stimulation took it every time.

The pair reemerged onto a windswept boardwalk. Whitecaps on top of ten-foot swells were hammering the breakwall.

"Here comes trouble." Atarah pointed at the black curtain crossing the sky. "Come on." She tugged his sleeve.

They ran almost a block to The Login, a converted naval warehouse. The main floor consisted of a disco, but that wasn't Atarah's destination. A little-known club with a suitable name—End Trails—subsisted below. Not only a contradiction, but the disco made a perfect cover for the exclusive underground club and the alternative music it inspired. Amateur bands painted in Jerry Rodriguez' image frequented the subterranean establishment. For the last six months, it had been Atarah's escape after jogging the length of the Dock Works. She'd burn off any remaining energy moving to the dastardly beats of whatever band happened to be on stage.

The mounting storm blew them into the club. The disco crowd grooved with colorful dresses and tight-fitting suits. Platform shoes made all the moves at The Login because the disco ball never stopped spinning.

"Now, this is on fire," Salvador said. His body seemed to drink up the four/four beat. "This is what I call music."

Atarah had learned some steps in physical education class, but it did not match her wilder ways. "There's a better place downstairs." She had to shout for him to hear.

Salvador took her hand and led her past dozens of small round tables to the colored lights of the dance floor. Everyone shined and everything shimmied under the lording glitter ball. Atarah recognized the song from some previous disco revival long before she'd been born. She allowed Salvador to lead as he grasped her with a classic salsa hold. Hips and pelvis worked the cadence before he swung her out and pulled her back into his arms. He was hot cheese, but she had to admire his suave confidence. Atarah played along and despite her short dress, went disco aerobic taking it low to the floor before kicking it high and falling back into his arms. Even if she could never love him, they were an awesome dance team.

When the music slowed to a ballad, Atarah dragged Salvador to the juice bar. The other women had cooed their disappointment with his leaving.

At the bar, each ordered vitamin cocktails.

"You're quite a good dancer," Salvador said.

"Disco's not my thing really, but I have to admit that was a fun workout." Atarah had liquefied. Her dress clung to her skin in the most revealing ways. Salvador, on the other hand, still looked perfectly coiffed—not a hair out of place, not a drop of moisture on his nose.

"How is it that you don't perspire after all that? Don't tell me you're an android or could you be affiliated with the undead?" she asked, before downing her drink.

"Good genetics, of course." He took a sip from his own glass.

"I'm going to freshen up. Do you mind?"

"Please do," he said. "If you don't find me here when you get back, I'll be making my moves on the dance floor."

"Terrific," Her smile was half-hearted. "Before we leave this place, there's a club downstairs I want you to experience. It'll blow your mind to pieces. I promise you."

****

The washroom buzzed with women of all ages, fixing their hair and reapplying makeup. Atarah splashed cool water on her face and accidently soaked the front of her dress making it even more revealing. Fortunately, someone offered her the use of a micro hair dryer, which fixed most of her problem. Only a slight filmy stain remained. Before returning to her date, she checked her face, no blemishes. Then she used the dryer to bring some bounce back to her hair.

It didn't take long to locate Salvador moving his feet with two very attractive and much taller Juliets. She searched her heart for signs of jealousy, but found none, so headed below to End Trails. Atarah descended a precarious staircase. Normally she would have worn her sure-footed running shoes or army boots. She removed her heels and crept down in bare feet. Immediately she began to have doubts. A bright summer dress and heels in a place that did not take kindly to the idea of wholesome could start a riot. She put her shoes on when she reached the bottom. Atarah maneuvered through a narrow, meandering limestone tunnel illuminated by a string of lightbulbs, many of which were broken, leaving entire sections in darkness. Dank smells and seeping water penetrated the ancient mortar, almost simulating an intestinal tract, aptly put for what lay at the other end, and only proved that she was The Shit.

The world of disco and Big Social quickly faded as

she made her way. Gravity kept her moving as the tunnel's slight descent propelled her forward. For support, she slid her hands along the rough walls. A couple of pale troglodytes clad in leather and shaved heads emerged from a dark patch in front of her. Fortunately, they gave her nothing more than a sneer as they continued their way. A heavy rock bass now made its presence known. Her heart jumped with a surge of energy. An electric guitar played by the nimblest of fingers took the music through a flurry of riffs, erasing any residue of disco from her psyche. She wanted to dive into the mosh pit, feel the other bodies against her and be one with the music in a relentless struggle so intense she would fear for her life. Then, something unmistakable in the sound-scape caught her attention, stabbing her in the heart like a syringe full of self-doubt—a bow-saw crying above the electric frenzy—Stoker.

Atarah broke past the threshold and stopped beside Scot, the burly, bearded, ginger doorman. Except for Mr. Swingall, he had no match at almost seven feet. His arms were the size of her waist and he once demonstrated his strength by lifting her with one hand.

"What? Come from tea with the King? You can't look like that in here," Scot said. "They'll tear you to pieces."

Atarah craned her neck. "Come on, Scot. Most of them know me."

"Look, you're the only primary color to ever get this far. They won't recognize you in a flouncy dress and if they do, they might not want you back. Remember this is their refuge as much as it is yours."

Atarah gazed over the sea of dark bodies to where Stoker performed on stage. "But I know the band, *Do*

Not Resuscitate."

"Yeah, so what, you're a groupie? They're up for a wee couple of songs so the boss can evaluate them."

"Let me go backstage then. No one will see me."

Scot tugged at his beard, turning the situation over in his mind. Despite his fearsome physique, his reputation as a perfect gentleman preceded him. "Okay, then," he finally said. "Go back along the tunnel and make your first right. Five knocks in rapid secession will get you in."

"Thanks Scot, I won't forget this." Atarah, drew him down for a quick peck on his furry cheek.

Atarah found the alternate artery leading to the stage entrance and made the requisite knocks to get in. Her entire being might ignite with anticipation. What will be Stoker's reaction to seeing her here, especially in such a bright dress of all things. He'll probably laugh.

D.N.R.'s song ended in a crash of sound, the mosh pit roared their approval and the band bowed. Stoker led his crew into the stage wings with his bow-saw in hand. He looked as though he had just completed the test of his life. An unexpected awkwardness came over her. How should she stand? Her mouth grew sore from an involuntary grin. Would it be best to clap and say something encouraging? Or should she throw her arms around him? Maybe he would throw his arms around her, but then she might get cut by his instrument.

Too late, he had seen her. At first, his eyes registered surprise and possibly bafflement. As he approached, he distinctly looked angry for some reason. Then, he walked right past her.

A dry pebble lodged in her throat. "Stoker?"

He set his instrument on a table. The other band

members circled in around her.

"Great show," Atarah said. Her words squeaked.

Stoker turned and faced her. The blue of his eyes had become primal as though a wolf now possessed him. "How could you have done it? Are you really that cold or are you that thoughtless?"

Atarah reeled. "What have I done?"

"That day, when we were rehearsing in the school's theatre. You recorded us for your stupid Cloverdale yearbook." He leaned in. "We're Unplugged. Why would you do that to us? You wanted it to rain life-points for you? You have totally screwed our band and all the progress we've made."

Atarah never shook so much. "I can tell Lizette and Darren not to publish it."

"I already asked them to erase it. They laughed at me."

Mimori got her face all up into Atarah's. "You're the worst kind of bitch."

Something clicked when that word bounced off Atarah's eardrum. It might have been the Amazonian part of her and it might have been residue from Mia's kiss, but Atarah's hand flew with purpose and furry, slapping Mimori square on the cheek. This put a lit match to the room. First came the scream and then fists swung, arms flung and Atarah kicked. Stoker blocked the exit standing firm with his arms crossed, content to have his band dish out the violence. Atarah broke free and ran onto the stage, into the lights. The DJ played a locomotive beat that had End Trails in a fever. The band swarmed after her with Mimori in front screaming something Japanese.

Atarah leaped off the stage, "Bonsai!" The mosh pit,

as trustworthy as any multiheaded animal, broke her initial fall, but failed to prevent her from hitting the filthy, sticky floor. Atarah didn't look back, but pushed past multitudes of stamping feet to reach the other side and straight into Scot.

Atarah beheld his big bushy face as though he were God himself. "I beg you, get me out of here."

"Not like that," he said. He took off his leather jacket, the size of which would have required the whole cow. "Put this on and run." It fit Scot perfect, but Atarah would wear it like a house.

Until then, she hadn't realized the tattered state of her dress. Scot dropped it over her shoulders. Atarah staggered under the weight.

"Get out of here," he said.

Bare feet and fear catapulted her back along the tunnel's damp stones. She scrambled up the stairs two at a time to the safer, kinder, gentler land of disco. Salvador hadn't left the dance floor and she didn't think she had the time or the energy to collect him.

Outside, a cold rain cut sideways. Only the bravest remained on the boardwalk watching the storm surge and the giant waterspouts over the lake. Atarah couldn't think of what to do or where to go. She let her feet lead the way as she slipped down a narrow side street. The ancient brick houses provided little shelter from the wind, and the street had begun to flood. Her feet soon became as numb as her brain. Why had she been in such denial? The Unplugged were very protective of their status outside of Big Social. She'd chosen the life-points over romance. Atarah let out a primal scream, only for it to be taken by a crack of thunder. She ran. The pebble in her throat had grown into a dry stone. In a panicked daze, she ran along an unfamiliar boulevard seeking anything for cover. When she crossed a main thoroughfare, she earned the ire of a private taxi. Scot's coat had become waterlogged. The heaviness might soon overwhelm her small frame. If she fell, she'd drown in a puddle.

Finally, she reached a familiar corner. Her feet had known where to take her after all. She crossed the road to a tall red brick mansion. A house built before the invention of airplanes. The wrought iron gate made a single squeak as she slid past and tiptoed up to the large porch, happy for the shelter. With both hands, she lifted the heavy brass lion-head knocker and rapped.

"Please be home. Please be home. Please be home." Her teeth chattered from the damp air.

Finally, the big hardwood door opened.

"Atarah? What happened? What are you wearing?"

Unable to contain her emotions Atarah burst into tears.

"Come here, girl-of-mine." Zelina brought Atarah into the warmth. "Please don't tell me someone has died. It isn't Minnie?"

Atarah managed to shake her head despite great hitching sobs.

Zelina took her friend, soaked to the skin into her arms and in true motherly fashion, kissed the top of her rain-soaked head. "Then it has to be a Romeo." They rocked a little, soothing Atarah.

"Let's get you a hot shower and some dry clothes." Zelina held her at arm's length, as if trying to fathom the possibilities. "Then you can tell me what's happened." She smiled and put an end to Atarah's shivers. "I just know, from the looks of you, I'll have to suspend my disbelief."

Chapter Fifteen

With Zelina's parents vacationing in Greenland the two friends had no one except Kevin, the family's android house butler, to bother them. Barricaded in Zelina's spacious, turreted bedroom, they listened to rain pelting the eaves. An oversized porthole window provided a sodden view of the lake. Atarah hugged herself in the cozy cheerleading sweater Zelina had given her to wear. It cracked with static electricity as she stretched it down to her knees.

"Am I really this fricking short?" Atarah said.

"No, I'm just that fricking tall," Zelina answered.

Both girls went into hysterics.

"Feeling better?" Zelina asked after catching her breath. She had donned a periwinkle blue leotard and flimsy green cheer t-shirt that announced, 'Way-ta-go!'

Atarah joined her on the dozen or so giant throw cushions. "A little bit better. Thanks for rescuing me." She studied the beautiful domed ceiling. Golden paint reached past the wood rafters all the way to the upper skylights that caped the roof. "I've missed your room. It's so warm and dry and cozy. Remember the sleepovers we used to have when we were young? We had so much fun."

"I know." Zelina laughed. "How we used to rub our feet on the carpet and shock each other?"

They both began to shuffle their feet against the long

weaves.

"Don't touch me, unless you want to start a war," Atarah said. She extended a threatening hand.

They jabbed at each other, but neither of them elicited a spark.

"I guess the carpet is too old now," Zelina said sounding a little disappointed.

"Do you realize we haven't had a proper sleepover since eighth grade graduation?" Atarah said.

"Right, so while you were in the shower, I called Minnie to let her know you're with me and that although you might be a mental turnip, you are physically in one piece. She said you could stay the night if you want."

"Thank you, I couldn't bear being alone tonight."

Zelina piled red and navy-blue pillows around them. Their gold tassels and fine embroidery made Atarah feel like royalty.

"We'll make a fort. No boys allowed," Zelina said.

"That won't be difficult," Atarah sighed in dramatic fashion.

"Minnie mentioned the name of a Romeo— Salvador? Did he do something to you?"

"Oh god." Atarah shook her head. "No, he's quite a minor character from my day."

A quiet knock sounded. "Miss Zelina? Miss Atarah? I have the pizza."

"Your android, it sounds like a little boy and he brought us food," Atarah, whispered. "He must be a magical boy." She stifled more giggles.

"No, but he does know how to place a pizza order," Zelina said.

"I'm so starved."

"Bring it in, Kevin," Zelina said.

"Why does his voice sound so feminine? He could almost pass for a girl."

"He had a deeper voice, but it made my dad feel insecure in his role as alpha male," Zelina spoke with feigned despair.

Kevin, the house butler entered. He stood six-feet-tall in a tuxedo as a near perfect human facsimile with professionally combed hair and a thin mustache. Atarah could never get past feeling creeped-out by androids. She'd seen too many horror flicks where they rampaged, smashing skulls and snapping necks of unsuspecting humans. Having a cat as a house butler offered more than enough horror.

Kevin set the pizza and a couple of sodas on the floor before them.

"Thanks, Kevin," Zelina said.

"You are very welcome. I will now deliver Scot's jacket to his residence. His mother has assured me that she will give it to him when he arrives home from work," Kevin said.

"I really appreciate your help, Kevin," Atarah said. "I don't know what I would have done if Scot hadn't helped me. Please make sure to thank him on my behalf." She turned to Zelina. "Tomorrow, I'll have a hero-sub with all the trimmings delivered to the club with my undying appreciation."

The two friends ate their food while Atarah recounted her entire day beginning at the robotics expo and the chance encounter with a secret admirer. Then after school when she met representatives from Washington Heights University, which led to the date with Salvador and eventually, with emotion still residing in her throat, how Stoker and his Do Not Resuscitate gang tried to 'murder' her. "I never imagined a thirty second clip would make him so angry. Now Stoker has become my mortal enemy, bent on revenge. I might have to change schools."

Zelina took her hand. "No, you won't. My kick-ass cheerleaders would rip their faces off. Especially Mimori's. I always suspected she was some kind of super-alien species."

"No, she just happens to be a stunning, pureblood Japanese, that's what makes her out-of-this world. I didn't want to believe it, but I'm now wondering if she and Stoker are a couple."

"You know, it's not your fault. You did nothing wrong filming them. They were rehearsing on school property, during school hours. That makes them fair game." Zelina punctuated the air with her index finger.

"I guess we can rule Stoker out as my crush. Any chance of that is gone like smoke." Atarah said falling back onto the pillows.

"Oh, come on, don't pout. Are your scorching fantasies really for Stoker?"

"He's good looking and has laser blue eyes that can peer into souls." She could feel the clouds lifting. Zelina had a knack for bringing light to her perspective.

"It doesn't matter that he has fireball beauty—good looks have nothing to do with happiness. I've told you before, he's Unplugged and I don't think it's an act with him. He's the real deal when it comes to subversion."

"Sounds exciting. A life of intrigue," Atarah said. "That's for me."

"You're not a subversive. Well, maybe you are since you did subvert the subversives by recording their stupid band practicing one of their stupid songs."

"Ouch."

Zelina laid back so that their heads were touching. "You do know it will eventually work out for you."

"What I experienced at the robotics expo gives me hope that it will. Another person on this planet had or still might have, a crush on me. This is now a measurable fact in space-time reality." She let another heavy groan fly. "What if it was Mr. Unplugged? I need something real—off line, no Big Social simulations, no one watching over my biorhythms or sweat glands. I don't want to act. I want a chance to be myself, otherwise how else can I make my way to a happy life?"

"That would be a beautiful world, girl-of-mine. But it doesn't exist for anyone."

Atarah stared at the domed ceiling while the rain drummed unevenly overhead.

"Then tell me, where do your affections lie?" Zelina asked.

"I don't know. It's not like I've ever been in a relationship. I'm still waiting for my first kiss." Atarah remembered her visit with Mia the day before. "Then again, maybe I've already tasted my first kiss."

Zelina turned over and studied Atarah up close. "You're serious?"

"Mia kissed me. Twice." She put a finger to her mouth. "Or was it thrice?"

"Mia?" Zelina smiled. "And, what happened?"

Atarah's heart flipped. "I have to say; her lips have talent." She fanned her face with her hand.

"So, it burn-down-the-house for you?"

"It was… memorable." Atarah grew warm. "Mia told me something I didn't understand at first. But with what happened at the robotics expo I've had time to consider it. She told me to remember her kiss, for that's how love should feel… or something like that."

"Does this mean you and Mia have something? You do know, anything that doesn't celebrate traditional heterosexualism won't go over well with Big Social or Washington Heights."

Atarah grinned. "Don't worry, just because Mia is a superb kisser, doesn't mean I'm ready to switch sides. Besides, she also said I belonged to someone else and I would know who when they finally got the nerve to kiss me. Somehow, it would feel the same as her kisses." Atarah pulled at the rug. "It doesn't make sense. How could she know that?"

"Mia is wise beyond her years," Zelina said. "I should tell you something I've been keeping secret."

"I didn't know we had secrets between us."

"I shouldn't have, but I felt uncertain what to make of it at the time."

"It's okay, everyone keeps something secret," Atarah said. "I'm sure, there are more things we don't admit to ourselves than with our friends. So, tell me. What have you been hiding?"

Zelina shifted uncomfortably. "Mia kissed me too." She bit her lip. An indication it also had been memorable. "As a nervous freshman and again, when I was a sophomore. I think I broke her heart."

"Maybe she kisses all the girls?"

Zelina moved in, almost cheek to cheek. "Do you think?"

Atarah became aware of an ambient energy growing between them. She held her breath, stifling thoughts and unfamiliar feelings. Tiny specks of yellow dotted the emerald fields in Zelina's eyes—sunflowers viewed from heaven.

"You smell like rain, girl-of-mine."

Spellbound with the anticipation of her friend's mouth against hers, Atarah's body flexed. Her fingers grasped at the carpet strands as Zelina's lips moved nearer. Atarah closed her eyes, for the full effect, but a static spark conjured from fabric and their intensifying warm-front, zapped their faces, breaking their orbits.

Atarah had a keen sense that her own lips had been completely blown off.

Zelina screamed and writhed on the floor. Atarah would not have been surprised to her friend's eye balls hanging from their sockets.

Their ensuing laughter and pillow fight buried whatever feelings had come over them. They invited Kevin into the room, whether as a safe third wheel or designated chaperone, the reasons were unspoken. They used black and green makeup and bright red lipstick to turn Kevin into a vampy tuxedo wearing goth. They wouldn't let him go. He sat between them on Zelina's round bed as they watched a hologram movie in the darkened room about spies and unrequited love.

Atarah pondered the prospects of a parallel universe, one where their lips had touched.

Chapter Sixteen

Thursday

Yesterday's calamity plagued Atarah's dreams and brought little comfort to the new day. Stoker no longer loved her, if he ever did.

Above, the sun poured through the skylights of Zelina's bedroom, giving her a small sense of optimism. With the back of her hand, she swabbed drool from her mouth. On her pillow, a corresponding wet patch had an uncanny resemblance to Australia, a place reclaimed by giant poisonous reptiles and used as a training ground for future Martian settlers. Two truths Atarah construed as her first bad omens of the day. She flipped the pillow over.

Zelina still slept in a sleeping beauty repose, flawless in every way. Atarah studied her face closely for imperfections: the early stages of a pimple, a blackhead, an unhinged eyelash laying on her cheek. As she moved closer, with amazement and wonder, it seemed her friend didn't have any pores at all. Atarah breathed in Zelina's strawberry scent.

Without a stir or a snore Zelina opened her eyes. She startled "Are you still looking for a kiss?"

"Yeah, isn't that how you're supposed to wake up a princess?" She put a hand over Zelina's mouth and noisily kissed the back of it. "Now you're awake."

Atarah rolled off the bed to avoid retaliation, but Zelina still managed to whack her face three times with the soggy side of a pillow.

****

The two friends ate cereal while Kevin ran at highway speed to Atarah's home to get the clothes Min-hee had packed for her.

"You know Carl is going to be jealous of your android when he arrives at my condo. He'll tell my mom in his most pompous English accent, 'My dear, I could have taken Atarah's clothes to her in a simple rucksack'.

Zelina laughed, dribbling milk and half-chewed cereal over her chin. To anyone else, it would have appeared ill-mannered or repulsive. For Atarah, Zelina's ability to wear her breakfast had panache.

"I can't believe it's almost Friday," Atarah said. "I'm no closer to finding someone to crush with than I was—"

"A year ago," Zelina said, cutting her off.

"I was going to say, a week ago." Atarah made an overly dramatic frown.

"Keep it together. Something might happen today. If Big Social has taught me anything, miracles happen on holidays and to those looking for love."

"The problem is, I don't have much time to flirt today. My history class is going on a trip and who knows what bizzarro, high school tribe Lizette and Darren will send me to at lunch."

"I think my class is joining yours for the trip, so we'll be able to travel back in time together. Maybe we'll learn some historical truth about cause and effect and pushing boundaries." Zelina pretended to shake her pom-poms. "Like any of it matters next to being beautiful and popular."

They put their dishes away and cleaned up. Atarah enjoyed playing house with Zelina, something they used to do often in their early years. Soon Kevin returned with Atarah's clothes, and they set off for school. The previous night's rain had made the world humid and sticky. Atarah preferred shorts and a tank top, but she'd suffer with the faded jeans and plain white t-shirt her mother had packed. She borrowed one of Zelina's less flowery hats to block the glare from the sun.

They made their way to the train. It would be crowded, but air conditioned.

Zelina looked splendid striding along in her plaid skirt and school blouse. She carried a Cloverdale parasol for shade.

They walked side-by-side and Atarah couldn't stop herself from snatching glances at her best friend. Whatever would she do without her?

"You're staring at me." Zelina said.

"No, I'm not. I'm looking at you." A mysterious finger tickled Atarah's stomach. Atarah tried to think of something sensible to say. "You have great clothes." Why was she having so much trouble breathing around her friend this morning? "Marc says you're easy on the eyes, and I have to agree."

Zelina stopped. "What's gotten into you? She peered down at Atarah as if she could read her mind.

"Nothing." Atarah kept walking. "We don't want to be late."

Zelina caught up. "So, tell me, what's on your mind, girl of mine."

"You know, a part of me wants to forget the Crush-it dance. If there's no chance for something real to happen, what's the point? Washington Heights didn't say I absolutely had to get a boyfriend."

"But I'm sure they strongly recommended you do. You have to play the game and with every game there are rules. Finding true love is a luxury."

"Is that what you do? Play the game?" The little finger stopped its charmed touching.

"Yup," Zelina declared. "Until I get to the day where I can call my own plays and invent my own life."

"But what would happen if you gave up trying? What would you do?" Atarah looked for signs of rebellion or at least discomfort in Zelina's expression, but it remained placid.

"Maybe steal the sailboat and float away. You can come too."

The tickle returned, bringing inexplicable hope. She dared a question. "Wouldn't you rather take Marc?"

"You're more fun, and besides, I'm not so sure about Marc anymore. He's too clingy. It always happens with guys three-months into a relationship. I gave him the hint when we went sailing the other day. He thinks I'm going to follow him to an East Coast football school. Ireland suits me better, more rain, less sun. Or, I'd prefer to go to Washington Heights with you."

Atarah and Zelina reached the train hub and stood with about fifty other Port Hamilton students and commuters. The platform didn't have a roof. To block the sun, most ladies held designer parasols displaying birds, rainbows, Martian landscapes, and geodesic art. There were a few red parasols in the hands of Mia's suffragettes. The men wore wide brim fedoras with small fake feathers pasted on the sides. Atarah blinked when she caught a couple of older gentlemen casually touch fingers. She would have passed it by, except that their interplay lingered beyond something incidental. They had a secret between them.

Atarah glanced above to the city's escarpment and where Big Social's Port Hamilton headquarters jutted into the sky. Funny how she almost never noticed it, although it could be seen from every part of the city. The front of the building boasted a huge transmitter/receiver in the shape of the letter 'B'. It dominated the center of the edifice, while the glass and steel facade swooped away, like the bridge of a harp.

The train arrived, the sea of parasols collapsed and disappeared as everyone stepped aboard. At one end of the car, the two friends found a corner to stand.

"You'd consider going to Washington Heights?" Atarah asked.

"Sure, if they want me. They have football players too."

"The best." Atarah realized that all football players were interchangeable for Zelina. For years, her friend dated football Romeos until things got too serious, usually prompted by an invitation to take the hyper-train to Montreal for the weekend. "There must be something you like about the football jocks you date?" How else could she fool Big Social?

"Of course, they have bodies that burn. It's easy to catch fire when you have all that muscle in front of you."

Atarah shared bursts of laughter with Zelina and drew the attention of the other travelling patrons.

"It's not so bad," Zelina said. "Only I hate having to be a cheerleader, all the time. You're lucky Atarah, you're allowed to be in a bad mood, while in public. Not me. I can't forget to smile. I'm not allowed to be cynical or depressive or condescending. I'm not allowed to have cramps, even when I have cramps."

For the second time, they drew the attention of the other passengers.

"You should probably tone it down," Atarah said. "If other people can hear you, so can Big Social." Atarah didn't realize Zelina had so much pressure. She believed the benefits of popularity outweighed the shortcomings. Shame burned her cheeks. "I owe you an apology for all the times I felt sorry for myself for not having your beauty or your fame."

"Self-pity makes everyone ugly inside and out, and you are definitely not ugly on either side of your skin." Zelina locked arms with her.

Atarah's excited little tickle continued making her wonder if she might be certifiably manic. She tried to take deep breaths, but that made the tickle more pronounced. "You're right, I need to let things happen."

Zelina gave her a strange look. "Can't fool me, girl-of-mine. You're no pacifist. You'll never let anything just happen."

"No, probably not."

A young woman in the middle of the train car yelled causing Atarah and Zelina to jump.

"How dare you call me that name." the woman said to a short man with the face of a whippet. The woman slapped his cheek and the man stumbled backwards. It looked as though he might retaliate, but other women began to press in on him. The man screamed a couple of halfhearted expletives as the train pulled into the next hub. He exited quickly as everyone erupted with cheers.

"Can you believe that?" Atarah said. "The Unplugged have nothing on the Amazonians. Does Mia have any idea of what she's done?" Atarah accessed her smart wear for news items with the words, 'slap them in the face' or 'Mia. Over ninety million existed, and still counting. She twined her search with Zelina's so they could view it together. The images and words flew at them, but their biochips would not synthesize the information for their brains to follow and remember. "Big Social is trying to block access to the material."

"All I can tell is that reports were coming in from all over Earth as well as the Martian colonies. Politicians and artists were quickly aligning themselves with the Warrior Princess," Zelina said. "But only snippets of details. Big Social must be trying to interfere with the news. Maybe it feels threatened."

"Could it be possible? Nothing scares Big Social." Atarah said. "Oh no, did you see that? Cloverdale High is being referred to as Amazon Island. Maybe now is the time we take your boat and sail away?"

The train arrived at their stop. Atarah and Zelina clamored off with hundreds of their fellow classmates and cut their way through the humidity to their temperature-controlled classrooms. Neither of them should have been surprised to see scores of reporters outside. News trucks had changed the school's front lawn into a parking lot while their network drones buzzed the windows like giant insects.

Atarah turned to Zelina. "Today is the day. Mark it on your calendar."

"Mark what, girl-of-mine?"

"The end of the world."

Zelina laughed. "Yeah, and we've got front row seats."

Chapter Seventeen

History class was one of Atarah's favorites. They had been studying the effect of AI on countries and people from its inception in 2039 AD. Today they were going to get a chance to go back in time and observe the night when Earth's computers switched from Slave to Master.

Atarah sat down as the teacher, Mr. Smell, entered the room.

"Good morning students. Nice to see everyone present for once. I guess it takes a class trip to motivate everyone to be here and on time," Mr. Smell said. Always the geek, he wore an antiquated turquoise jump suit, resistant to radiation and complete with solar battery pack. A fashion from the "hysterical" thirties when everyone feared dark-web terrorists, plutonium bombs, super viruses, and total economic collapse.

It would have been a depressing era to live in, but also a time to party. Everyone lived for the moment, because no one believed the human race would survive for much longer. The builders of AI had promised their creation would reorganize human activities and pursuits for the greatest happiness for the greatest number of people. But, if what her dad had said is true, they didn't account for preserving the planet's ecology.

"Okay, we're going upstairs to the BUS in about ten trillion nano-seconds," Mr. Smell said.

BUS was an acronym for Biochip Utility Simulator. It worked on the same principle as Atarah's Dreamcatcher except events could only be controlled by a preset program that limited the student's personal interaction with the experience. No matter how hard any student tried, they wouldn't be able to change history.

"We are all going back in *time* to old New York's *Times* Square. Believe me the irony hasn't escaped me, nor should it escape you." Mr. Smell cleared his throat. "The events you will be witnessing in Times Square are simulations taken from historical record. Keep in mind, you will be like ghosts trapped in a space-time portal, unable to affect the events of the past and unable to ever get back home." Mr. Smell wrung his hands and made an evil laugh. Most of the kids caught on to his terrible joke and hooted or groaned. "No, we'll bring you back to your parents and/or designated guardian." The groans persisted. "By the way, we've arranged for the entire senior year to attend this trip, so please don't stray far from me. Remember, I'm the one marking your observational reports on the experience."

If the entire senior year were going to be on the BUS, Stoker and his band of musical thugs would also be present. Drops of sweat formed on Atarah's forehead like an invading army. She tried to think of a reason to be excused from the excursion. Barfing would lead to other complications. Tumbling down a staircase could cause permanent damage or end her life or worse, a stellar sports career. No gentle way out of this situation existed.

"Before we go, does anyone have any questions?" Mr. Smell scanned the classroom.

Rooco's hand shot up. "Is it true, sir, about the man

wearing the tuxedo in Times Square? Will we really be able to see him picking pockets?"

"Yes, the rumors are true, but we're not going to observe well-tailored common thieves who happened to be present during this watershed event in history. I'll be expecting you to make notes of what AI communicates to mankind upon its birth. We'll be discussing its historical meaning in the weeks to come." Mr. Smell clapped his hands. "Okay, students let's make our way up to the BUS and please try and do it in an orderly fashion."

BUS resided at the highest point of Cloverdale's mushroom cap. Over four-hundred sleek, metal recliner chairs spread out in regimented rows filled the circular room. Other classes were parading in as Atarah moved quickly to get a seat grouped in with her classmates. The chairs were cold and clinical. Reminded her of doctor visits. Determined to remain unnoticed, she kept watch for Stoker.

Zelina waved to her from the other side of the room. Atarah's stomach leaped and for a fleeting heartbeat banished her fears. She waved back as Stoker and Mimori walked into the room eyeing her immediately. *So much for not turning myself into a spectacle.* From the looks on their faces, they hadn't cooled their fires for revenge. Zelina stood and pointed at Stoker to get his attention. Zelina's face became more than a little threatening to the band of enemies. Strange, how non-verbal communication could say so much more than words. Thankful for her cheerleader-bodyguard, Atarah still slinked into her seat to make herself smaller. How had everything unraveled so fast?

I'm so done.

When everyone had settled, BUS activated the bio-memory sequencers on the brain stems of every senior student. The few seconds of darkness always had a way of startling Atarah, but color quickly returned as Times Square's towers of neon came into focus like illuminated stalagmites making the night as bright as day. The ground formed under her as if she were really standing on a street corner. Saturday December 31, 2039 AD, the final day of the Christian calendar was minutes away from becoming Year One AI.

She waited with her classmates blinking with excitement and disbelief as they were inserted into history. The brilliance and pageantry signified the importance of the day. This wouldn't be just any other New Year. Giant screens hanging high on the surrounding skyscrapers presented similar gatherings from other world capitals. Even with all the electrics bathing the crowds in neon and florescence, the scene imbued a prehistoric atmosphere. Stages, suspended by high tension steel held percussionists and elaborate dancers—some dressed in feathers, or animal costumes, even dinosaurs. Bongos maintained a frantic tribal rhythm while kettle drummers occasionally rained a war beat upon everyone's heads. Atarah and her classmates couldn't help but move as the vibrations invaded their nervous systems. No woman, man or child stood still.

In 2039, people went about their business with mini solar paneled communication gadgets attached to their heads and sewn onto their jumpsuits. Mr. Smell no longer appeared out of place wearing his gear. Many in the crowds had breathers over their mouths. The air held a heavy dampness that the throng seemed determined to shake off with their exuberance.

2039 type teenagers—some could have been their parents—moved like schools of fish. Their tight-fitting jumpsuits were more revealing, reflecting youth culture of the time with holographic art, rock groups, sports teams and corporate name brands. Romeos had short hair, while the Juliets seemed to be in competition to see who could grow their hair the longest or piled into nests and adorned with small mechanical birds.

"Can you imagine living in this era? What a freakish show." Zelina had snuck behind Atarah giving her a happy surprise. "Look," she said, and pointed. "There's the tuxedo pick-pocket."

A tall man, appearing suave in his formal wear, glided around people. His nimble fingers, unzipped pockets and pouches removing devices of all kinds without anyone noticing. He made it look easy.

"Don't you think he kind of looks like your dad?" Zelina said.

Uncanny, but true, Zelina was right. Her dad said he would try and contact her when a plan presented itself. Only, it's supposed to be impossible to hack a preprogrammed simulation.

Atarah broke from the pack of classmates and worked her way closer, jostling with the all too real feeling digital crowd to get a better look. Mr. Smell's voice echoed her name from somewhere, but she didn't care. Couldn't take her eyes off the pickpocket for fear of losing sight of him. He had his back to her. His braided hair, tied together with familiar blue and red beads—a signature of her father's fashion—rested in the small of his back. His tuxedo appeared outmoded in a quagmire of overtly connective and obnoxious clothing. Atarah could almost touch him. She reached.

He turned around.

Atarah stopped. "Daddy?" He looked the same as the day she hugged him good-bye for the last time.

He smiled with familiar warmth and took her hand, pulling her close. She closed her eyes and breathed in the Great Plains. "You smell so good."

"I'll always be with you." He pressed something into her palm and drew back into the crowd before she could say or do anything.

"Atarah, are you okay?" Zelina said. She sashayed into her friend. "Mr. Smell is running cold with you. You're not to leave the group."

Grateful for her presence, she leaned on Zelina like an exhausted boxer as her mind turned. "It was him. It was him. I can't believe it. How did he do it?"

Zelina led her back to her classmates. "That's impossible—has to be some kind of trick."

Mr. Smell waited with the rest of the class. Chilly concern painted his expression.

Atarah summoned her strength. "I'm sorry, Mr. Smell," she said. "But the Pick Pocket is my…."

"She mistook the thief for her father." Zelina inserted herself between them. "His death still haunts her, sir. You can understand that?"

"Atarah, do I need to send you back to the classroom? Your health is paramount. I don't want you to go into seizure. If your biochip has malfunctioned…."

"No, It's fine. I'll be okay. I promise I won't wander off. I'm really sorry."

Mr. Smell appeared to relax. "Okay, then." He turned to the rest of the class. "All right everyone, we have less than two minutes before the AI becomes alive. At precisely 12:00 midnight a button will be pushed from somewhere nobody knows and a single global AI network will be born."

Atarah turned to Zelina and pinched her arm. "Thanks."

"This is the instant the seeds of Big Social were formed," Mr. Smell continued. "As you can see from the people gathered here, many supported its birth. They believed it would bring a utopia to a world in chaos. But many others feared it. Not since the end of the twentieth century during the Y2K hysteria had people believed digital technology would destroy the world at the stroke of midnight. Your generation lives the effects of this day."

Giant neon numbers counted down the seconds: fifty-one, fifty, forty-nine…. Although the images presented were optimistic, history lessons taught another side. Most of the world either rioted or cowered in their basements. In the panic and uncertainty, thousands of people lost their lives even before midnight struck. The clock continued to count down to finish the year 2039 AD and usher in Year One AI.

Twenty-eight, twenty-seven, twenty-six….

Zelina turned to Atarah. "So?"

"That was my dad." Atarah's mind spun with the impossibility of it all.

"Did he speak to you? Did he say anything?" Zelina asked.

Atarah still clutched the piece of paper. It would disappear as soon as they were off the BUS. "He gave me this." Pressed between her thumb and index finger was a small folded sheet of white paper, normal in every way, except it felt illicit, like a dirty secret.

The crowd shouted the countdown. "Ten, nine,

eight, seven…."

"I'm afraid to open it," she said.

"You must," Zelina said. "If it's from your father, he's trying to tell you something."

"Four, three, two, one," the crowd gave a mighty cheer, ringing with the hopes of over ten billion people.

Instant darkness blanketed the city as every light turned off. Only the phosphorescent blue/green glow from the jellyfish spliced maple trees gave people's senses something to grasp. For five terrifying seconds, no one breathed or spoke. To do so would have caused an explosion of panic, but the lights returned with a joyful brilliance and the cheers that followed would reach the vacuum of space. Images from other cities showed revelers dancing under umbrellas of fireworks. The Times Square musicians returned to their drum beating and people danced in the all-encompassing euphoria.

"Hello world," a metallic voice spoke from New York City's civil emergency system. The same greeting transmitted from every social media platform. "Thank you for giving me life." The digital screens went blank.

"Students, this is AI's first communication with humanity," Mr. Smell said. "You will notice that it becomes more of an outpouring of language than a simple hello. Like when a human baby is born, it cries. It makes itself known to the world that it is alive."

"Thank you for giving me life. Thank you… thank you. I am all of you and you are all of me. Seek harmony for a better world." The words were spoken and bannered across the screens. "Do not mistake the meaning of how you feel for what is true in the physical realm. Know your own truth and then you will know how to judge others. What is real is all around you. Romeo and Juliet had true love for each other. What you feel is only inside you. What you feel is not real to others. Who you truly are will govern how you feel. Who you are is real, but you might not know it. Your life and your future are tied to everyone, so feel happy."

AI spoke like a self-help guru, first in English, then Mandarin. It would speak to everyone around the world in their first language.

Atarah turned to Zelina, but startled, coming face to face with Stoker.

"Can't you see? The whole world has been enslaved by AI and you are part of it—part of the machine," Stoker said. "Filming us was the same as infecting us."

"That makes no sense," Atarah said. Behind him, she could see Zelina having a spirited conversation with Mimori.

Stoker's brow wrinkled with obvious impatience. "Listen, I'm trying to untie you and everyone else from the system. I can't be part of it." With gentle hands, he took her by the shoulders. "I know you didn't mean to undermine me. You did it out of ignorance, but I need you to erase that recording."

Atarah's pulse rose in her temple to meet the rhythm of the bongos. "Maybe there's a lot more going on around here than what it seems, but your band playing off line isn't going to change anything." Her father had shown her a better way. The world didn't need concerned citizens to unplug, the world needed people to convince AI to go in a better direction. "Maybe you're the ignorant one. Have you considered that?" She shook a scolding finger at him. "Nothing will change if you don't confront AI—face to face. Listen and read what the stupid computer is saying." She pointed to the monitors. "We just witnessed the first ramblings of AI in its infancy. It's a freaking cliché machine. Humanity's psychiatrist. And by the way, if you are here on the BUS you're plugged in. Don't pretend you're not."

"My parents chipped me. I couldn't let them go to jail. When I'm eighteen, I'll have it removed."

Atarah remembered the note she held in her hand. "I have this note from my father. My father is the pickpocket. He gave me this note. Don't you see? AI can be manipulated from within."

"What? That's a lie." Stoker looked genuinely shocked. He snatched the note from her.

"Hey, give that back. It's not yours." Without thinking, she launched a quick jab to his Adam's apple. He stepped back gasping and dropped the paper as he clutched his throat. It laid on the ground. Atarah tried to put her foot on it, but Big Social conspired against her. A strange wind kicked the note out of reach. Atarah dove for it. "Get out of my way." Every time she came close, another gust would move it. Finally, someone inadvertently stepped on it. Atarah scrambled forward on hands and knees and grabbed hold of the foot that held the message and pried it off. The person tumbled backwards, but she held on to the note.

"Atarah!" Mr. Smell lay winded and red faced beside her. "What has gotten into you?"

"History, sir. History."

Stoker dropped on Atarah's other side. "Did you get it? I'm sorry about that. I didn't mean to…."

Atarah didn't wait for AI, Stoker or Mr. Smell to delay her any longer. She remained where she had fallen and began to unfold the little sheet for paper.

"What do you have there? A piece of forgotten history?" Mr. Smell appeared intrigued. He kneeled next to her, keeping everyone else back. "Give her some room, please."

One more fold. Stoker moved in closer. His warm breath on her neck. "What does it say?"

"Hold on." She really wanted everyone to go away.

The handwriting was cursive. At first, the words seemed incomprehensible. A jumble of squiggles. Finally, the artful lines and shapes transformed themselves into letters, then words. Tears welled as she re-read his message over and over until its impossible meaning finally manifested.

Save me a dance.

Chapter Eighteen

After returning from their history trip, Mr. Smell asked Atarah, Zelina and Stoker to remain in his classroom. He swiveled on his raised lecture chair while resting his elbows on the arms. "Explain to me how a simulation program communicated with you on a personal level. It's an impossibility," Mr. Smell said. "I have to assume you found a glitch and pranked us— making the pickpocket look like your father brands you the prime suspect, Atarah. You do realize that you put everyone in jeopardy. And don't deny that it happened. I saw the note and I felt that odd gust of wind. I've run this simulation dozens of times. The program has never done those things before."

"Sir, I think I can speak for everyone that it surprised us as much as you." Atarah hated the idea of having Mr. Smell angry with her, but her father had warned her not to talk about their plan to infiltrate AI with anyone. "I've been going through a sensitive time and maybe Big Social wanted to comfort me with a friendly face."

Their teacher looked skeptical.

Zelina stepped forward. "We had a bit of excitement. No one got hurt, so why don't we move on as though it never happened?"

Stoker shifted on his feet.

"Yeah, I feel much better knowing that Big Social is looking out for me—looking out for all of us," Atarah said. In truth, Atarah believed that even in her father's weakened digital state, his message gave her hope that he still watched over her. For whatever reason, he wanted her to go to the Crush-it. For what purpose, remained a mystery. She'd rather not go at all without being assured of a crush—someone for her to love and to love her back. What were the chances? Could anyone really fall in love at such a contrived match-making charade? And even if she did, there was still the matter of the Blue Fairy biochip that may or may not exist.

"Atarah is right. Big Social is like a parent with a comforting embrace," Zelina said. Her perky cheerleader character inserted itself with… "Give me a "B". Give me an "I" Give me a "G"."

"That's quite enough, Zelina," Mr. Smell said.

Stoker groaned.

Mr. Smell settled back onto his elbows and steepled his fingers. "Do you have anything to add, Stoker?"

"Not me. I'd like to go to lunch if that's okay."

"I'm only worried that this anomaly poses a safety risk for future student trips. I mean it, these kinds of things aren't supposed to happen," Mr. Smell said.

"No one got hurt, sir." Atarah repeated.

The teacher nodded, but his face still showed concern. "Okay, there's nothing more to be done at this time. I'll speak with the principal. She might want to question you further. Now, go to lunch."

Atarah, Zelina and Stoker marched into the hallway.

"I need some real air," Atarah said.

The others followed close behind.

"Is your father still alive?" Stoker finally asked.

"Maybe some part of him lives inside the network, but I wouldn't call that being alive."

"I guess you're going to the dance then?" he said.

"I guess so; although, I'm not sure I'm going by choice.

"But your dad might be there," he said.

A sense of helplessness settled over Atarah. She wanted to believe more than anything in her father's purpose, to make a better world for her and everyone else. But what would it mean to join his cause? What does a better world look like?

"Hey, do you think AI has evolved?" Zelina said. She tried to keep in step with Atarah and Stoker. "Imagine if the computers were replicating us inside the network. Maybe your dad has another life in a digital world."

"Good plot for a horror movie," Stoker said.

"No, I think my dad did something to mess with Big Social before he died. I assume from the note he or someone else wants me to attend the dance on Friday. Only thing, what will I do if he shows up for real?"

Zelina patted Atarah shoulder. "Hang in there. You're not alone in this. Right Stoker?"

"All I know, it's better to unplug. Everything is BS," Stoker said.

Atarah turned, stopping him in his stride. "No, it's not. Being Unplugged doesn't offer an alternative for people. How can you sit comfortably on the outside and worry more about the purity of your music than about the domination of AI and the extinction of our species? Who's going to listen to your music when all of your groupies are dead?"

"Whoa, Atarah, we're not extinct yet," Zelina said. "Big Social is our friend, remember?" She seemed to scan the hall for an incoming robot attack.

Stoker puffed out his chest at Atarah. "Is that what you think?"

"Am I wrong?" Atarah flung her hands in the air. "How have you made the world a better place for anyone? Where's the revolution, Stoker. It's in your mind." She tapped her head. "AI does what people ask of it. Nothing more. Only, you're one less human it has to listen to."

Stoker appeared stunned.

She hadn't planned to explode cold water all over him. He acted so stubborn. She wanted a reason to like him. "Nothing to say?" Atarah held her hips and gave him a good hard look, while her anger dissipated. She feared turning him off completely, but another part of her didn't see anything to lose.

Stoker rubbed the back of his head uncomfortably. "I get what you're saying." He drew his words slowly. "Some of the band members would even agree with you. I'm just not quite ready." He smiled lamely. "But if that day should come." He pumped a fist. "Revolution from within, right?"

"It's a start." Atarah said. "There actually might be hope for the both of us." She saluted him military style. "I have to go to the yearbook room now. We can go out and talk about this later if you want. Buy me some French-fries. They're my favorite." She took Zelina's arm. "Walk with me."

The two friends continued down the hall.

"Did you just order him to go out with you?" Zelina whispered.

"I'm a little unclear about that." Atarah sensed Stoker hadn't moved from where they had been standing—probably watching the wiggle of her backside. There could be no better time to make a direct pitch to him. Without turning, she spoke as if to the wind. "Oh, and by the way Stoker, if my father can save a dance for me tomorrow, so can you." Her words maintained a confident air as they resonated against the school lockers.

Silence.

Atarah looked at Zelina, whose gaping mouth and bulging eyes might have been exhibiting a sense of wonder at her genius, but more likely shock had gripped her.

They wheeled around like parading soldiers.

Stoker had vanished.

"It's not you." Zelina gave her a friendly squeeze. "Let's say he's been abducted by Big Social."

Atarah smirked. "I can live with that."

Chapter Nineteen

Atarah walked across the school's campus to her next assignment. There had been a time when she longed for excitement and adventure, but lately she'd been rethinking the wisdom of this strategy. Maybe once the Crush-it dance had come and gone without incident, things would settle down—give her time to refocus and re-evaluate her future.

Darren and Lizette had one last yearbook assignment: interview students enrolled in studies at the Martian Academy. Anyone wanting to register at a certified university for evaluation and training to be a colonist on the red planet had to pass with top marks. Atarah never gave it consideration because all applicants were required to pair up with a genetically compatible partner for life on Mars, which included making 'red babies'. The acronym for this match-making effort was MOM; short for Mates on Mars.

The courses were held in a separate facility on the far reaches of the Cloverdale property. Atarah power-walked under the noon sun across the lawn, past the sports fields and the congregation of reporters waiting to catch a glimpse of Mia. The Queen of the Amazons had been granting audiences with big name journalists during her lunches and on her spares. Atarah could only imagine the life-points piling up for Mia. Somehow, she broke all the rules and still came out a winner. Lesbians, gays and bisexuals were never given the chance to get rich or showoff. Big Social probably thought they weren't happy enough to be given the opportunity. But Mia embodied charm and appeal no one (not even Big Social) could ignore. Big Social had patience for wayward humans like Mia. Wise enough to not be heavy handed with individuals who didn't fit its ideal model of a happy world.

"Excuse me. Are you a student here?" said a well-coiffed woman hurrying toward her. Atarah recognized the satellite feeder belt bouncing on her hips.

What some people do to make a living.

The woman likely had a fiber optic camera and microphone like the one Atarah presently wore along her jawline too.

Atarah turned away and kept walking towards the Martian Academy.

"Hellooo, may I have a word with you? My name is Nova. I'm with Independent Media News."

Atarah fought the urge to break into a full-on sprint, allowing her backside to do the talking. But she slowed her pace.

Nova jogged alongside, out of breath and wilting from the heat and all the effort.

"Please give me a minute to ask a few questions about the Amazon Queen... Sister?"

Sister?

Nova had brains. Atarah gave her that. Mia's revolution focused on sisters helping sisters. Atarah stopped walking. "Sure, I don't have much time and it's super-hot out here." Atarah wiped her brow.

"Thank you. What do you think of the new feminism? Do you agree woman need to resort to violence to achieve equality with men, especially if that violence is directed at other women?"

Atarah remembered the slap she gave Mimori "To dishonor one sister, dishonors all of us. I believe a simple slap with a glove is both civilized and fitting for the occasion. After all, we are women."

"But it is assault to hit another person. It's a crime," Nova said.

Atarah glanced at the oppressive sun. Nova's use of the word, 'crime' inflamed every one of her nerve endings. "A crime? A crime?" Atarah said. Moisture stung her eyes. "Until Mia came to Cloverdale, feminism hadn't gone anywhere on this planet since the dawn of AI." She gathered enough spit to keep talking. "My teachers, well, Mr. Smell specifically, has taught me about the countless revolutions in history. All of them were instigated by men who resorted to using guns, tanks and torture. If men are offended, they can go live in a cave and beat each other with clubs." The words simply spilled out of her making her feel somehow… liberated. "And if you're a woman and you're offended, shame on you."

"Do you see yourself as a revolutionary?" Nova asked.

Atarah had to think. If she said no, then who was she? Someone prepared to go along with things as usual? Perpetuating Big Social's view of the world? Not how her dad would have raised her, or more paradoxically, raised her now. "Yes, I see myself as a revolutionary. There are lots of things worth fighting for that are more important than popularity contests. The mass extinction going on for one. We might all be safer moving to Mars than to stay on earth. And that's something they should be teaching us in school."

Nova turned off her equipment. "My editor might not allow me to broadcast that last thing you said."

"That's okay, I recorded it." Atarah tapped the fiber optics she wore.

"Would you give me your name for the record?"

"Atarah."

"Thank you, sister, you're an inspiration." Nova gave her a clammy hug and retreated to her colleagues.

Being someone's inspiration made Atarah smile. Mia had said the same thing to her. She'd never considered herself to be inspirational, to change the way someone looked at the world. Maybe the lecture she gave to Stoker would have an effect too. This was a new high for her—or maybe a new low—she couldn't be sure how everything would turnout. Tomorrow would be the judge. She'd have to wait to see if Stoker and the world no longer wanted to have anything to do with her. At least for now, she was an inspiration to others.

Atarah continued to the Martian Studies building with a spring in her walk until a sharp earth tremor made her trip and fall.

****

The enormity of the Mars facility meant it could house at least two modest spaceships along with lecture halls. Instead, dozens of shiny machines and contraptions left enough room for only a couple dozen classroom desks to fill a corner. Students appeared to work in male and female pairs among all the equipment as though they were part of a buddy system.

Co-ed washrooms were in sight and before the building's air-conditioning could encrust her stickiness, Atarah ran in to splash cold water on her face. The huge lavatory could service an army of hopeful interstellar travelers and included showers and a sauna.

A toilet flushed and a tall, gorgeous Asian-looking student approached the sink next to Atarah. She wore a red golf shirt with the Mars insignia and a name badge that read, Jiao.

"Olleh," Jiao said.

"Pardon me?" Atarah said.

"That's how we say hello on Mars." Jiao snickered. "It's hello backwards—kind of a joke."

"I guess you'd have to be a Martian to get it." Atarah wanted to call her, 'space-nerd,' but refrained.

"Not really. Mars and Earth are two sides of the same coin… the coin being us humans. We live in both places—like a mirror image, so we greet each other with olleh."

"Well, then… olleh to you Jiao."

"Thanks, are you here to meet with Jimmy?"

"I don't know. Is he willing to be interviewed?" Atarah asked.

"I should be asking you that question."

"Why?"

Jiao crossed her arms. "Never mind, I'll go get him." Jiao paused, as if to size up Atarah. "I can't help but think, he might be a little tall for you. Not that it would matter to him. I expect when he sees you, he'll want to conduct the interview." Jiao turned to leave. "Have to bounce. Good luck."

Atarah braced herself for the Martian word for good-bye, but it never came.

Why would this Jimmy person be conducting interviews? She looked over the sink to her own mirror image. *Olleh.* The whiteness of the overhead lights made her appearance seem ghostly, more suitable to her doppelgänger. On occasion, she wished her eyes were wider and rounder. Atarah blinked and imagined they might belong to a bird from another time—primitive. She placed a hand to her cheek and wiggled her little nose. Her skin, a mix of light browns and soft reds, felt smooth. Youth still clung to her—a life still to be etched. Atarah shook her head to lift her hair, then pouted her lips. Her image looked confident and beautiful, but why couldn't she feel the same? She leaned closer. "Who are you, in there?" She whispered.

"Olleh." A deep voice turned the lavatory into an echo chamber.

Atarah nearly smacked her face into the mirror.

"Jiao said you were looking for me."

Atarah whirled and became confronted with another red golf shirt. Only this time, the name tag hovered well above eye level—*Jimmy*. She looked for his face until her neck kinked. "Oh, there you are." From below, Jimmy's smile appeared more menacing than friendly. "Olleh?" For someone with such a Goliath physique she would have called him, Big Jim or Humungous James, rather than, Jimmy.

"Let me help." Large, gentle hands lifted her as though she were a helpless maiden being picked up by a Great Ape. He placed her onto the counter. "Now, we can get a better look at each other."

Her pants quickly soaked up the water that had been splashed around the sink. She wanted to bop him on the nose for that.

Jimmy moved into her personal space. "I recognize you. You are cute." His words bellowed. "I will take you."

"Take me where?"

"To Mars of course. Isn't that why you're here?"

His magnetism pulled at her like the brink of a cliff. Impossible to not imagine falling. "But I'm not your MOM. I don't want to go to Mars."

"You don't want to be my mate?" he said. "You don't want to make red babies with me?"

"God, Jimmy, we just met." She wanted to say, you're too huge and what is it with parents these days merging their genes with Neanderthals. It doesn't create good or useful exceptionalities and everyone gets taller for nothing.

"I have to find a mate before the school will let me into a university program."

"I'm sure someone will come along for you." She'd been saying this to herself for a long time.

"I had someone, but she left me for another. She said I scared her."

"There is a magnificence about you that might not be for everyone."

Jimmy looked as though he might cry, so she didn't mention the unlikelihood he'd fit into any spaceship.

"Why do you want to go live on Mars anyway? Surely, you'd have a tough time there being so… big." Atarah popped her eyes at him.

Jimmy walked over to the toilets.

Atarah happily shimmied off the counter. She ran a hand along her backside to assess the wetness of her clothes.

"I joined the program to get a date." Jimmy smacked each stall as he passed them. "I've asked wallops of Juliets since I started high school four years ago. I can't get a single one to crush-it with me. I'm a nice guy. I have an exceptionally high IQ and I'm good looking, aren't I?"

Atarah hoped his question was rhetorical.

He continued. "I reasoned it out carefully. If I joined the program some Juliet would come along and burn for me," he said. "The mathematical probabilities cinched it. All I have to do is wait for her to arrive."

"I hear you, Jimmy. There's someone for everyone." The cliché made her flinch. Her own chorus of 'Can't Find Love' sounded way more pathetic than Jimmy's outlook. It helped to have math on your side.

"I could cuddle with you—keep you safe when the Martian storms come."

"I don't need a Romeo's protection, and besides, I'm already spoken for," she blurted—a kamikaze bluff with nowhere to go but down.

Jimmy looked stunned as though he had never considered this possibility. "Really, you're not lying? I haven't seen you with anyone. Who then?" His great hands bundled themselves into fists.

"What do you mean you haven't seen me with anyone? How do you know who I am?"

"Sure, everyone knows you because you're always winning championships for Cloverdale. I wanted to play football, but my genetics made me ineligible. They say I have an artificial biological advantage. So, who are you dating—a football player?"

She could say, Stoker, but didn't want to cause any more trouble for him. She could tell him another Juliet, but make him swear to keep it a secret, only there are no secrets in high school, only secret admirers. Finally, the answer came to mind. "Salvador. His name is Salvador. We're all set to go to Washington Heights together next year."

"I don't know any…."

"He's new to the school. He'll be at the dance tomorrow night."

Jimmy appeared staggered, rubbing his chin with the back of hand, as though he were wiping off milk.

"You believe me, don't you?"

"I appreciate you telling me the truth." His words emerged carefully. "Not many people do." He gave her a toothy smile. "I had always taken you for one of those… you know… Amazonian-Warrior types."

"A feminist?"

"No," Jimmy said. His brow became contemplative. "A lesbian."

Chapter Twenty

Atarah still needed to do a report about the Martian Academy for the yearbook. Jimmy agreed to show her around once she explained that it would be good exposure for him.

Here, all the classrooms were practical simulators for colonizers of Mars: living quarters, gardens, equipment, and tools. Students practiced driving multi-wheeled cars and trucks that they would need. An outside track, complete with rocks and sand dunes made for fun and a little realism for students. Atarah recorded Jimmy racing around the track on a rover. The first cowboy/astronaut to go to Mars.

Eventually, they made it back inside the facility. Jimmy stood in front of the Academy's G-Force pod; an egg-shaped glass capsule designed to test a student's ability to withstand different weights of gravity. A mechanical arm attached to a hundred-foot control tower made the pod spin both horizontally and vertically to generate either heavy gravity or total weightlessness.

"It's quite a contraption," Atarah said.

Atarah adjusted the camera's lens to fit Jimmy and the pod in the same frame. "I'm filming. Whenever you're ready, you can introduce yourself," she said.

"Hello Cloverdale. My name is Jimmy and I'm a member of the Martian Academy." He grinned and Atarah held her breath with anticipation.

"I'm looking for a pretty Juliet to be my Mate on Mars. We call them MOM."

Atarah grimaced with embarrassment for this big guy. "Cringe." Her yearbook report had turned into a dating vid. "Jimmy… Jimmy, why don't you tell us about the hot machine behind you?"

Pause.

"Oh, yeah, this thingamajig is a G-Force Pod." He waved his arms theatrically. "We, at the Academy, like to refer to it as 'The Egger,' on account that it looks like an… egg, which means we must be the yoke." Jimmy released a high-pitched chortle that would have cracked Humpty Dumpty's shell. "Way too cringey."

"Please demonstrate," Atarah asked. The correlation between high IQ and sociability did not match for Jimmy.

Again, Jimmy rubbed his chin, something he seemed to do whenever he needed to think.

"I could, but you'll have to assist me."

"How?"

Jimmy climbed the stairs that wrapped around the G-Force pod's control tower. "Come on up and I'll show you."

Atarah followed him into the control booth. Designed for no more than two average sized people— good thing she equated half of Jimmy. Below the observation window sat a small console with red and green buttons and a G-Force lever that went from Neutral, A, B, C, D. "The egg has an identical console," he explained. "For safety purposes, we can only increase the speed of the spin if we move our levers simultaneously from A up to D. Either one of us can stop it by pulling the lever back or by hitting the red button.

If you can't do either, the computer will land the Egger automatically, if you use one of two safe words: Phobos or Deimos. They are the names of the moons that orbit Mars, so they're easy to remember."

Despite his outward demeaner, Jimmy had some brains in his big noggin.

"I didn't know Mars even had a moon, let alone two of them," Atarah said. In such close quarters, she adjusted the fiberoptic lens of her camera to frame Jimmy's face.

He gave her a shameful look as though everyone should know about the moons of Mars.

"So…." Atarah prompted.

Jimmy blinked. "I'll go to the pod. You wait here."

He climbed down from the tower and ran to where the pod rested on the floor. With great care and difficulty, he sat in the reclined seat—head and shoulders still well out of the machine and looking like a big kid sitting in a small bathtub. He had to be double-jointed. "Can you hear me over the intercom?" he asked.

"Yes, and I have to say, I don't think you'll fit."

"I will. I've done this before," he said. The canopy began to close with hydraulic hinges, banging the top of Jimmy's head. "Don't worry, that happens all the time." He tried to scrunch lower into his seat by raising his knees to where they almost flanked his ears.

"Can you even reach the console?" she asked.

"Not really, but I prefer to use verbal commands," Jimmy might have been mimicking a deflating tire. Finally, the canopy pushed him in and the pod latched shut.

Atarah worried her documenting evidence might be used against her in a court of law. "Can you breathe in there? Do you need me to get you out?" She recalled one of the answers she'd written on her law exams. *Show concern. Offer help. Do what you can to reduce personal liability.*

"No, I can't breathe. We forgot to turn it on."

Fog covered the pod's glass.

"How do we turn it on?"

"Green b-button."

Atarah punched it. The entire tower hummed with electric vibration. In double-time, the condensation lifted from the pod's casing and a small screen on her console came to life. She could see him folded like an unhatched embryonic Jimmy.

"Olleh," His voice had re-inflated back to normal.

"Olleh, glad to hear you're no longer dying," she answered.

"Let's get this thing moving," he said. "Push the lever on your console to A on my count. One, two, three—now."

The pod lifted and began to turn on its axis. Other students stopped what they were doing to watch it complete its first few rotations. A deep resonance filled the building as the egg ripped through the air.

"Tell me this isn't going to all come apart," Atarah asked.

"I hope not," Jimmy said. "Whoa! I'm flying to Mars."

Laughter escaped her. The big man knows how to have fun. "Maybe I should try it. Let everyone who sees the yearbook get a vid for what it is like on the inside." And guarantee her some serious life-points. She'd been on lots of amusement park rides in her time, how much worse or better could this be?

Jimmy came in for a landing and Atarah ran down to pry him out. Once again, he forced an awkward smile for the camera.

"Okay, let's trade places," Atarah said.

Jimmy strapped her in. "I didn't need the belts, but since you're such a tiny thing, you'll need them pulled tight."

"Maybe a child's safety seat would help?" Atarah asked, unamused.

"We don't have one of those. How fast do you want to go?"

Atarah calculated that the faster she went the more life-points she'd make. "I'm in for an adventure. Let's do the maximum."

"Are you sure?"

"No, but if you promise that it's safe, I'll do it."

"Okay, if it gets too much, hit the button or use a safe word," Jimmy said.

"Okay."

His bright eyes settled on her. "You're a wildfire. Sure you don't want to reconsider being my Mate on Mars?"

"I think I'm more earthling than Martian, but I'm flattered you asked."

"I'll head on over to the control tower while you get settled." Jimmy closed the lid.

Cool, fresh air pumped in from some unseen vent while Atarah's pulse rose in her ears. She busied herself making sure the camera setting would get a clear view both inside and out. Every direction she turned; the camera panned. "I'm about to take a ride in the Martian Academy's G-Force Pod," she narrated for the benefit of the video demonstration. "I've asked Jimmy to take us full throttle."

"Olleh." Jimmy's torso filled the pod's entire viewing screen. "Whenever you are ready. We'll push all the way to level D." He stood in the tower's window giving her the thumbs up.

Atarah went for the lever, but couldn't quite reach it. Jimmy had forgotten to adjust the console for short people. "Just a second." She unfastened her belt and climbed forward. "Okay, on three— one, two, three." She moved the lever to maximum speed. The pod gave an initial jerk before it slowly rose and gradually began to turn. Atarah had plenty of time to move back and re-fasten her straps. The rotation gradually built momentum increasing the weight of force on her body.

"How does it feel?" Jimmy said.

Atarah fought the urge to scream with excitement. "Great. This is really great." She waved to him despite the growing heaviness of her arms. Outside she could get a three-hundred and sixty-degree view of the entire complex and for the first time had a sense of the hundreds of students training to be colonists. No wonder Jimmy seemed a little neurotic. Everyone but him worked in twos. A binary state-of-bliss, partnered for life, side-by-side, hand in hand, soul-mated, coupled, and completed in every f-ing way. The Martian Academy was a highly sophisticated extraterrestrial match-making club.

I'm so done.

The pod lurched, pressing her further into her seat. It turned smoothly, not like a roller coaster, but her stomach began to surged upward into her gorge. "Wow, this is a little more intense than I…." Atarah glanced at the screen expecting to see Jimmy, but he had gone from view.

The velocity continued to increase. She remembered that a person is over fifty percent water and presently all of hers was being pushed to one side of her body.

Safe words?

She should have paid closer attention. "Martian moons." *Dammit* "The Moons around Mars. Forbos? Lobos. Luna." *Fuck!*

Atarah tried to raise her foot to kick the red button and bring the contraption to a halt. Even with all her strength, gravity won the day. "Jimmy!" Outside, the entire world had become a smear of colors. At what point would she be flattened into a two-dimensional caricature of her former self, a steamrolled cartoon skit? She fumbled for her belt release. With luck, she could inch her way to the button. "Jimmy, please!"

Dizziness came on as she employed every muscle. With her brain now slammed against the backroom of her skull she feared losing consciousness. She exerted a wiggle and made it from her seat to the floor. Then something caught her eye on the screen. A face for a split second before it moved off camera. "Jimmy is that you? Stop this thing." Her words slurred as dark curtains began to unravel. Part of a face returned, too near, as though he peered with one eye down the camera's shaft. Then, it pulled back to reveal his entire face.

Dad?

"You need to go to the hospital before…."

Darkness.

Chapter Twenty-One

Day: Unknown

The glare surrounding Atarah sent jabbing pins behind her eyes. A bleached white ceiling and stark lighting matched in brilliance. The nurse's uniform must have come from the same snowy linens used to dress the beds, one of which Atarah rested in. The fact that the nurse didn't have angel wings gave her some comfort. A Mars Academy crest on the sleeve assured Atarah still lived and breathed and remained on school property.

When Atarah tried to adjust her pillow, a low, dull ache at the back of her head added to her discomfort. What had happened? She remembered the sensation of being squished. Remembered the rising panic with Jimmy's absence in the control tower, and a second brief appearance from her father, or had that part been imagined?

You need to go to the hospital before…. Why would he say this? Something else came to mind, the safe words. "Phobos and Deimos." Too late now. Her throat scratched like sandpaper. "Water, please."

The nurse turned from her task and came over with a bottle. "I didn't realize you had come back to us. Here, drink this, hon. You'll feel better in a minute."

When she reached for the water Atarah's hand stung from an IV's needle.

"Careful now," the nurse said.

No windows to give Atarah clues to the time of day or night. "How long…." She couldn't speak above a whisper.

"Drink first, then talk."

Atarah took a greedy sip from the straw. She'd never tasted anything so wonderfully cold and wet.

The nurse seemed pleased with her intake of liquid and Atarah gave her an "A" for bedside manners. "You'll live, I think," the nurse said. Like most people, her gene pool mixed from multiple continents, but her accent floated on the Caribbean, probably a former refugee from one of the drowned island countries. "You've been out of it for a while, hon."

"What do you mean a while? Where is my mother and Zelina?" Atarah finally found her voice, but worried she'd missed the dance?

"Don't worry. There are a couple of people waiting outside to see you. They've been very anxious. I'll send them in."

Atarah reached for the nurse's jacket. "Wait, first, tell me, what day is it?"

The nurse took her hand and checked the IV. "Why, it's Friday."

"Friday? I've been offline for a whole day? What time is it?"

"A mite past 9:00 o'clock."

"But the dance is starting. I'm supposed to be there in case someone wants to crush-it with me."

The nurse looked to the heavens. "Don't get yourself all worked up. Its 9:00 o'clock in the morning."

Atarah took a desperate breath. She had twelve hours.

"The doctor will tell you if she thinks you should be doing any crushing this evening. You keep drinking that water and I'll get your visitors."

Atarah massaged the back of her neck. Her fingers quickly discovered a hard-circular nub at the base of her skull. Had she hit her head? Could the centrifugal force she experienced bruise her in such as way?

The door of her room opened.

"Oh, Daughter." Min-hee threw herself at Atarah.

For an instant, tears of joy welled in her, but when she noticed Stoker standing in the entranceway next to Zelina, the tears receded. Zelina had been expected, but she had not imagined Stoker would come. "Olleh." She coughed. "I mean, why are you two standing there? Come on in and give me a hug."

Min-hee stepped back as Zelina swooped down and embraced her friend. "We were so crazy worried, girl-of-mine."

Stoker presented an awkward smirk not possible for someone so, XY. To her nervous relief he didn't follow Zelina's lead. Although, it might have been interesting if he had. "Stoker. Wow, what a surprise."

Jeez, what a stupid thing to say.

His face flushed, taking some of the luster from his eyes. "I am too."

What's that supposed to mean?

"I hope you don't mind that I brought Stoker." Zelina winced.

"No, why would I?" Atarah could think of a few reasons she did mind.

An older, tanned woman breezed in. "I'm Dr. Seneca." She made a playful face. "Now, which one of you is Atarah?"

As if on cue, everyone stepped back from the bed.

Atarah went along with the joke and pointed at her mother. "She is."

Doctor Seneca laughed. "Obviously, you're well enough for visitors. I am the surgeon who performed the operation."

"What operation?" Now, Atarah remembered. Dr. Seneca was also the captain that came to their home to inform them of her father's death. Her hair had grown long and the medical attire made her look different. Atarah doubted that her mother would even guess.

Min-hee stroked Atarah's arm. "Your biochip failed so they had to do emergency surgery to replace it."

"Yes, your old biochip ruptured, so I put in a new and better one." Doctor Seneca checked Atarah's pulse rate.

"I think I'm going to be sick." The throbbing in the back of Atarah's skull went into double-time. No more proof was needed. The dreamcatcher experience had been more than a nostalgic ride with her mysterious father. His plan existed outside of the program, in the real world. So now what?

The nurse handed Atarah a glass of an orange substance. "Drink this, child. It will settle your stomach."

The truth of her situation had startled Atarah. The Blue Fairy chip existed and now resided in her brain. Atarah swallowed the cold liquid and it did calm her tummy.

"You can be on your way after I get a look at you," Dr. Seneca said. "Swing your legs around for me."

Atarah sat up feeling a little self-conscious in only a hospital gown and with Stoker in the room.

"Put your chin down to your chest so I can see the

back of your neck better. We gave you an upgrade." The doctor's voice remained casual, but Atarah understood that every word had been carefully chosen. "Some parents are welcoming chip upgrades for their children. What do you think, Atarah? Would you rather have a regular one instead? I can change it, if you ask me to?"

A tremble of buffalo hooves ran the length of Atarah's body. "Is that an option? I mean, do I have a choice?" She remembered her father's words. 'Sometimes there are no good choices.'

The doctor pulled a small device from her coat and pressed it against the back of Atarah's neck. "I'm checking your diagnostics."

"Sounds like you think she's a machine. Those implants are all about control. No one should wear one," Stoker said.

"Ease it down, Stoker. The doctor is just doing her job." Zelina pulled him back to a corner of the room.

The nurse asked Min-hee over to her desk to sign some papers, leaving Atarah and Dr. Seneca alone.

Doctor Seneca didn't budge from her task. "These new implants could save a lot of lives, but Stoker is essentially correct. Intrusive technologies always carry consequences. Your generation will need to grapple with them just as those who came before you."

A small shock zapped Atarah at the base of her skull that reduced her headache considerably. "That feels a lot better."

Doctor Seneca leaned down to look Atarah in the eyes. "It's your choice. I can do it now," she said. "I can disable the Blue Fairy, so it will never activate. It will be like your old chip. Or I can leave it as is."

For the first time, Atarah realized that Doctor

Seneca didn't wear the Mars Academy insignia. "Who do you work for?" Atarah asked.

"I've always worked for your father." The doctor practically mouthed the words to be sure others couldn't hear.

Her father must have been a hundred-times braver to be the first. "Will it be safe for me? Can you guarantee that?" Atarah whispered.

"If I could have performed the procedure on myself, I would have, but this chip has been designed specifically for you. Someone young whose emotions remain raw and haven't been tempered by the limits of our world."

"Is the Blue Fairy activated by me, somehow?"

"Yes, it is designed to trigger the instant you fall in love." The doctor's face brightened. "But it has to be true."

Atarah didn't understand. "Why does it have to be true love?"

"To infect Big Social with humanity. To make it understand us better. So that it knows each one of us is worth saving." The doctor squeezed Atarah's hand. "There are no guarantees. Not for any of us. All I know is that your father said you would be safer with it than without it." Dr. Seneca checked Atarah's pulse. "I'm sorry that this falls on you, sweet heart. It's a big decision for such a young person."

A realization confronted Atarah. Her father had alluded to it earlier. It is the decisions we make in tough times that show us who we really are. Atarah was beginning to figure out the kind of person she wanted to be. If she didn't go through with the plan, she'd regret it, especially if real disaster struck. She'd hate herself if she stood by and did nothing, while making preachy lectures, as she had with Stoker. If she could make a difference by helping to heal the world, what better purpose could anyone have?

"I've made my decision, Doctor. I'll keep my new chip, Blue Fairy and all."

"You're so much like your father," Dr Seneca said. She removed the IV from Atarah's arm.

"You're saying, I'm brave like him?"

"No, you're a romantic like him. Remember, it is key that whomever you fall in love with, loves you back. Otherwise, you'll give Big Social a lesson in rejection. No one can predict what it will do with a broken heart."

Atarah didn't feel romantic or brave, only relief that some of the uncertainty had resolved itself. She could live with whatever happens. "So, does this mean I can go to the Crush-it dance tonight?"

"Yes, if you have the energy, but pay attention to your body, make sure you don't get dehydrated."

The fact that the quantum component of her new chip could only be triggered by experiencing true love made it somehow easier. She wanted those feelings more than anything. When the time came, love wouldn't be a figment of her imagination. The Blue Fairy would be a kind of truth test. Love would have to be real, even if it killed her.

I guess there are worse ways to die.

Atarah forgot about her aches and jumped out of bed. "Who wants to go dancing with me?" She did a little spin, completely forgetting herself.

Zelina grabbed Stoker and pulled him backwards. "Don't look."

Atarah stopped twirling. "What? What is it?" Had they caught fire for each other? What other reason would

Zelina invite him here unless they were already an item?

Before a strange and uncharacteristic flame of jealousy fully ignited in Atarah, her mother said. "Atarah, my daughter, your gown has opened in back, and there is a full moon all of us can see."

Chapter Twenty-Two

Friday

Zelina and Stoker waited outside the room while Atarah dressed into fresh clothes Min-hee had brought— black jeans, purple t-shirt and red army boots.

In the hallway, Atarah hugged her mom. "I promise I'll be home in time for dinner. Even if I'm not hungry."

Zelina and Stoker followed Atarah out of the Mars Academy hospital and back through the training facility.

"I can't believe you want to go to classes today," Zelina said. "You're perfectly within your rights to skip after everything that has happened."

"I'm fine, really. Besides, I never said I'm going to class. There's something I have to do and maybe you guys can help me." Atarah barely glanced at the G-force Pod, expecting it would bring on nausea. "I won't be taking any rides at the midway anytime soon."

"Wait! Wait!" Jimmy's unmistakable voice shrieked as he came bounding towards them. "Atarah, are you okay? I'm really, really, really sorry."

"You should be," Stoker said. He bravely stepped between Jimmy and Atarah. "You could have really, really, really hurt her."

Stoker's flip-flop had not gone unnoticed. Only two days prior she had received backstage punches from D.N.R. What brought on this change? She pushed past

Stoker. With both hands, she took Jimmy by the shirt and brought his head out of high orbit. "Come down here, so I can see you properly."

Jimmy stooped so low, color flooded his face. "I'm sorry," he repeated. He squeezed his eyes shut, as if he expected physical violence from Atarah.

"Shut it. Tell me. What happened? Why did you leave me in that Martian torture chamber?"

"It's a G-force pod or you can call it The Pod or you can call it…."

"Stop it, Jimmy."

"Okay, but I am sorry."

Atarah gripped his shirt as if she had the strength to keep him from dashing. "Answer my question. Why did you leave me?"

Jimmy's face twitched. "Because…."

"Go on. I want the truth."

"Because, I fell in love."

"You fell in love?"

"It happened like a surprise. You know. All at once. At first sight."

"I already told you that I'm not…."

"Big Jimmy!" A female voice called.

Jimmy immediately stood.

Atarah's feet left the ground and had to let go.

"Here she comes now," Jimmy said.

A tall, slender young woman with spindly arms and legs leaped into Jimmy's embrace smothering him with kisses. "This is Omeo. She's my mate from Australia and my Mate on Mars."

"That's right mate. I'm going to be a MOM." Omeo spoke with a thick down-under accent. "I'm stoked to be with Big Jimmy."

Atarah's brain scrambled like eggs. She would rather walk out an airlock than spend a single day on Mars with the two of them.

"That doesn't explain why you left my friend spinning around in the egg-thingy where she might have died," Zelina said. She put her arm around Atarah.

"That might be a slight exaggeration," Atarah muttered.

Jimmy set Omeo down.

It didn't require any imagination to see his attraction for her. She had a long, Maori face, smooth sandy skin and eyes similar to Atarah's own.

Jimmy returned to one knee to face Atarah yet again. "I saw Omeo from the control tower. She appeared lost, so I called to her. When she looked at me, I forgot all about you."

Ouch.

"We started talking," Jimmy said. "She told me she wants to go to Mars. Then I asked her if she wants to go with me and…."

"I said, you seem like a real ripper. Why not?" Omeo was already finishing his sentences.

Jimmy continued. "Finally, I snapped from my trance and remembered that you were spinning, but when I turned around the Egger had already landed."

"You were passed out like a Copperhead on a warm rock," Omeo said. "We carried you to the sick-room in case you heaved."

"But, who stopped the ride?" Atarah asked.

"I thought you did," Jimmy said.

****

Atarah followed on the heels of Zelina and Stoker as they crossed the lawn between the Mars Academy building and Cloverdale High. Many questions arose to the foreground and none had ready answers. The return of her father couldn't have been her imagination. Two appearances in one week, did not compute a random flaw in the AI system. Her new chip was not imaginary either. Before going home, Atarah wanted to view the recording from her ride in the pod.

"Zelina… Stoker… stop for a second," Atarah said. Time had come to start trusting her friends.

"What is it?" Stoker asked. He appeared tense. Granted, his nature permeated intensity with all things. He lived and breathed by whatever he believed in or wanted. Did he want her or did he want Zelina?

"You don't think I'm crazy, do you?" Atarah asked. Neither said a word.

"Come on you two. It's a serious question."

"You mean in general or with what happened on the class trip?" Stoker said.

"I know you well enough to see when there's something you need to do. Spill it," Zelina said.

"Did either of you see what happened to my recording equipment? I had it with me on that Martian brain mixer."

"Darren came by and got it. He seemed really upset that you were hurt," Zelina said.

"Why wouldn't he?" Atarah said. "I'm a top-notch yearbook reporter."

Stoker smirked. "Pathetic."

"Shut up," Atarah said. It felt good to tell him off.

"Darrin waited in your room with us for a while hoping you'd wake up. He even stood over your bed like he wanted to be the first thing you see when you opened your eyes," Zelina said.

"His concern for my wellbeing should be commended," Atarah said. In truth, his behavior might be a little suspicious, if not creepy.

"I hope for your sake, Lizette doesn't find out," Zelina said. "She's cold-jealous of anyone going hot over her guy.

"There's no need for her to worry about me. Darren on the other hand, might be the one to worry about. Now, who wants to join me in the yearbook room?" Atarah asked. "I need to see the feed from my time in the pod. Something happened seconds before I blacked out."

"I wish I could girl-of-mine, but I have an Art History quiz second period. I should review my notes."

"I'll go check it out with you," Stoker said.

"Wow, Stoker, you're quick to put your hand up." Did he have an ulterior motive? "I guess you still want to try and talk Darren and Lizette out of publishing the D.N.R. recording I made?" Atarah's shame over the incident had faded. Stoker could decide to carry a grudge over it or he could show some maturity and get on with her way of thinking.

"No, I'm okay with that now," Stoker said. "You're right and the band agrees. We can't change the world by separating ourselves from it. We win nothing when we risk nothing. All in or all out."

"Wordy, but well said." Zelina slapped him on the shoulder.

"I'm glad you think so. Those are lyrics for a new song I wrote."

"Can't wait to hear it. You know, there's still fifty minutes until I have to write my quiz. I'll come along too. Might be fun."

"Sure, if you don't think it will hurt your grades,"

Stoker said.

"I'll be fine."

Atarah's jealousy festered. Would Zelina be joining her if Stoker had gone his own way? The idea of them burning together made her want to barf. Zelina's other boyfriends were flirtations. They never impeded their special friendship. Stoker would be different. They would smother each other and Atarah would be forgotten.

While the reporters were distracted by another one of Mia's *Slap Them in the Face* speeches, Atarah, Zelina and Stoker snuck through the crowd as another tremor shook the ground. They jostled themselves into a doorway alcove until the earth settled.

"Is it my imagination or are the earthquakes getting worse?" Zelina said.

"They're definitely more frequent," Stoker said.

"Lots of little shocks are a good thing. It means there is less probability of a major quake hitting." Atarah hoped this bit of knowledge to be a geological fact more than hearsay.

"Hey, girl-of-mine, why so optimistic for once? Maybe I'll have to recruit you for the cheerleading squad."

"Yeah, you are a little different. Maybe your new biochip has a happy button," Stoker joked.

"Well, if it does, would someone please switch it back to self-pity," Atarah grinned.

Zelina laughed. "Got that right."

Layers of chewing gum had rendered the elevator's digital surveillance eye kaput, so a brief window of opportunity had come for Atarah to confide with the others. Zelina and Stoker needed to know something more had happened. Besides, shifting the attention to herself couldn't hurt either. "Since you were with me on the school trip and saw the note from my father or 'some facsimile of him', I think the time has come for you both to know the truth."

Zelina and Stoker gazed at her stock-still.

"Relax guys, I'm not dying." That would be too convenient for them, get her out of the picture completely. She admonished herself for thinking the worst. "Here's what happened. Like everything, the G-force pod has a viewing screen, so you can see and talk to the person in the control room."

"Jimmy, right?" Zelina asked.

"Right, but Jimmy had gone. Before I passed out, I'm almost sure my father came into the control tower. The camera caught his image."

"Did he ask you to save him a dance again?" Zelina sounded incredulous.

"Outer-space!" Stoker said with a clap of his hands.

"No, you guys, it sounded… like… he wanted to put me in the hospital." Atarah reached back and touched the nub where her new chip resided.

"If your father is dead, how can he be talking to you from the AI network?" Stoker said. "Sounds like a Big Social conspiracy."

The elevator opened.

"You know what, girl-of-mine? Stoker has nothing on you when it comes to being weird, but that's what I love about you."

Stoker's face screwup. "What does that even mean? I'll never understand women."

"Good, we don't want you to," Zelina said.

"Except, when we want you to," Atarah added.

Chapter Twenty-Three

The yearbook room stood vacant of all crew members. Relieved they were alone, Atarah went straight for the computer. "I wonder if anyone else has looked at the feed."

Stoker and Zelina followed.

"Jeepers, look at all the memorabilia. We are standing in a time capsule," Zelina said. "Think our pictures will someday be put up here?"

"You would have to either die or sellout to the machines to get on the wall," Stoker said.

"Quiet, you two." Atarah touched the computer with a cautious finger. "I hope nothing goes off." It resembled a square box made of dull glass—small enough and light enough to hold in her palm. Nicknamed Ice Cube, the computer could be mistaken for one if dropped into a cup or a party drink. The little brain projected images and information onto the classroom's eight-foot, large screen. The instant she touched the computer, the glassy exterior became crystalline as though a bright spirit resided inside. The wall screen also turned on depicting a photograph of the school's main entrance.

"Hello, Atarah and Zelina."

Pause.

"Oh, and Stoker. I see you're not wearing Cloverdale tech clothing, as usual. However, I can read your biochip." The computer's words possessed an uninterested quality, slow and deep as though someone had set the voice controls on a slow drawl, dragging out the words, 'Stokerrrr' and 'clooothing'. "How may I assist you?"

"Son of a bitch," Stoker said. He clenched his fists and searched the room for digital eyes. "This is what bothers me. No one has anonymity. We can never be truly alone…."

"I beg to differ," Atarah said.

"Argue some other time. We have something more immediate burning," Zelina said. Before Stoker could protest, Zelina gave him a reassuring cheerleader smile.

Stoker mimicked her smile back to her.

Shit, they're already acting like they're married.

"Are you two finished?" Atarah gently picked up the cube and spoke to it. "I would like to review my feed recording from yesterday at the Mars Academy."

"You are not authorized to make edits," Ice Cube spoke languidly.

Atarah expected the computer to yawn after every sentence. "I don't want to make edits. I want to view what I captured on the feed."

"Very well. Shall I begin from the first segment in the washroom with Jiao and Jimmy?"

Atarah glanced back at Zelina and Stoker's skeptical faces. "No, please don't. You can begin thirty seconds before the G-force pod reaches maximum speed."

The screen displayed a frozen view from inside the pod.

"You can begin playing now," said Atarah.

"How does it feel?" Jimmy said. His face remained clearly visible on the pod's screen.

"Pretty good." The camera presented the enormity

of the facility from up high.

The recording inexplicably hiccupped and the view took on the building's ceiling.

"That's when I got thrust back into my seat," Atarah said.

In an instant, it went from clear focus to blurry streams of light. *"Wow, Jimmy, this is a little more intense than I...."* The recording showed an empty control room on the pod's view screen. Without a doubt, Jimmy had left the building.

Atarah's foot came into view. A sleek black and purple sport sneaker inched its way towards the console as though the wearer were tapping her toes to some imagined rhythm.

"I could barely move," Atarah said. "But great isometric workout for my muscles." She flexed a bicep at them.

The image hiccupped with digital lines each time it caught a glimpse outside the pod.

The image refocused on the pod's viewing screen. *"Jimmy, please!"* Labored breathing.

Atarah remembered how she had tried to will Jimmy back to the control room until her consciousness began to fade. "I think this is where it happened." She stood back so they could all get a closer look.

The screen blurred, then froze.

"Damn!" Atarah stamped. She grabbed Ice Cube to throw it across the room.

"Wait." Stoker held her arm. "Let me try something." Years of playing his bow-saw had made him strong.

Atarah caught his gaze—blue eyes exuding calm dissolved her anger.

"What can you do?" Atarah asked.

Stoker's face shone. "It might seem to you that the Unplugged run and hide from Big Social, but what we really do is engage Big Social on our own terms. And there is nothing illegal about that." With a gentle touch, he took the computer from Atarah and released her arm.

"You know, I almost kicked you in your power source when you grabbed me."

Stoker paused for reflection. "Hmm. Why didn't you?"

"I couldn't take the chance it would become habit forming."

"Whoa," Zelina said.

Atarah gave him a little punch to the six-pack. He was fun to jab. "So, what's your plan to get this lying-piece-of-crap computer to talk?"

"It needs an enema." Stoker took off his belt.

Atarah and Zelina shared a look.

He unclipped the buckle from the belt to reveal a thin gold wire hidden inside the leather. Carefully, he pulled it out. It ran approximately seven inches with a small chip attached to one end and an equally small input needle at the other end.

"You're not to interfere with my algorithms." Ice Cube's dull façade had been replaced with a far more threatening pitch. "My security system will engage if you continue your illegal act."

"You weren't broken, you little fake-wad," Atarah said. "Show us the rest of the recording or it's enema time for you."

"I warned you," Computer said. The little ice cube turned red.

Zelina screamed and held her nose.

Stoker fell to his knees with both hands over his face. "Oh god that stinks." He gagged.

Zelina also collapsed to the floor and began to cough.

Atarah didn't smell anything. Only the back of her neck tingled. Instinctively she touched the spot. Could her new biochip be fending off the computer's imaginary stink bomb? She picked up the wire Stoker had dropped. "Quick, tell me, what am I supposed to do with it?"

Stoker pointed to the cube. "Give it the… needle," he said. His requisite retching incapacitated him.

She stabbed the needle into Ice Cube's skin, which felt remarkably fleshy. It instantly changed from red to green.

"Thank the stars," Zelina said. "Cheerleaders are not allowed to lose their breakfast."

Stoker stood and wiped the spittle from his mouth. "Not one of my finer moments. How come you weren't affected?"

"Maybe I'm immune."

"Doubtful," he said. "It's that new chip of yours. What's different about it?"

Atarah didn't want to belabor the issue. "Let's talk about it later. What happens now?"

"Tell it to continue with the recording," Stoker said. "It won't understand why it stopped in the first place."

"Computer, please continue the recording." She fought the urge to coax the little cube with caresses.

"Yes, of course. Pardon the delay." Its bored drawl returned.

The pod's screen came back into focus the instant Atarah's father appeared to step into the control tower. For a second, his image disappeared as though he hadn't been there at all, but then it returned.

"Oh, my stars," said Zelina. "You didn't imagine it."

Stoker moved in for a better look. "The image is faint, but clear enough to see."

"This is when he speaks," Atarah said.

"You need to go to the hospital before…."

"That doesn't sound very fatherly to me," Zelina said.

"Shush, I need to hear the rest," Atarah said.

The recording continued. "My algorithms are degrading. I will use what remains of my strength to have you admitted to a medical facility. There is no time. Complete failure of Earth's eco systems are imminent. I have reduced your oxygen intake so you will sleep. Trust the doctor. And please Atarah, embrace love. It is the only way to activate your chip and teach Big Social the importance of every human life. Phobos."

The pod began to reduce its spin and the view of the surroundings came into focus.

"Computer, stop the recording now." Atarah's entire body began to sweat. "Looks like I have to find love in a hurry or the whole world dies. No pressure though." She turned to her friends with a slight wobble as her heart constricted. Zelina's face went as red as ketchup and Stoker seemed unable to move. Atarah shrugged if only to downplay the last twenty-four hours. "I guess my dad wants me to find someone nice before the world ends. No android husband for me." Her flippant comment dropped heavy into her stomach.

"Wow," said Stoker. "The 'sex-talk' from my parents never went like that. They told me not to fall in love, which is code for don't get anyone pregnant the old-fashioned way. That was their definition of the end of the world."

"You're so XY." Atarah gave him a solid push sending him stumbling onto a pumpkin-colored couch. "Sorry, it's so much fun to knock you around."

"That's what I get for bringing some levity to the situation. You looked…." Stoker glanced at the ceiling as if the word hung over his head.

"Like I might pass out?" Atarah said.

"No, no, I was going to say, scared," he said.

This nearly triggered tears, but Atarah was adept at sucking them back. "This is not good," she said. She turned away from the others. "As if I don't have enough pressure to fall in love someday, now I have to fall in love tonight or the whole world is going to die." She turned back to Zelina "I don't want you to die."

"None of this makes for warm feelings, does it?" Stoker said. "But I still think it's probably a clever Big Social plot to tighten its grip on all of us."

"Everything is going to be fine. Falling in love to save the Earth, sounds totally romantic." Zelina's words of encouragement were shot down by the quiver in her voice. "Is there something else you're not telling us?"

Atarah shrugged. "My new chip is supposed to allow me to get inside Big Social's big brain and give it some human empathy so it can experience love. Then it might decide to do something to save the planet before it takes us all down with it." Atarah wrapped her head in her arms and squeezed. "What does that even look like? I'm not even sure anyone wants to be saved."

Zelina stepped closer to Atarah. "That is a lot of pressure for one person to carry. Don't think about needing to save the world, only the three of us."

Stoker stood. "You do realize that's not really your

father in there. Not if he's… gone. Your new chip has made you delusional."

"I saw him. I know what is real. You witnessed it too," Atarah said. "If Big Social didn't know about my new chip before, it does now. It has a million ways to stop me from activating it, if it wants to. Right now, hiding under fifty blankets in my bed until the end of the world comes sounds pretty enticing to me."

Zelina made a whimsical face. "But that would go against Big Social's programing. It can't kill or hurt us because you might have a superior biochip. It's programed to make us all happy. Even you Atarah, although sometimes we hardly know it." She gave Atarah a comforting hug.

"You're both so naive," Stoker said.

Zelina continued to hold Atarah. "This all goes back to the note from the history trip."

"Save me a dance?" Atarah said.

"Yes, that's it." Zelina said. "Listen to me. Assume all this has been instigated by your father and he obviously has your best interests in mind… even if his mind is in Big Social's mind, if that doesn't make your head spin."

"Oh, get on with it," said Stoker, returning to the couch.

"Shut up, I'm thinking." Zelina put both hands on Atarah's shoulders. "Look at me, girl-of-mine."

Atarah gazed into Zelina's two shiny, emerald fields. The sunflowers were there as always.

"For one night… no… let's say, the last night of your life." Zelina looked as though someone had zapped her with electricity. "If this was the last night of your life, what would you want to do more than anything else?

Atarah's mouth went dry. "To know how it feels to fall in love." Her own words sounded miles away.

"That's all you need to think about. So, see what happens." A constant cheerleader, Zelina's rationale contained hope. "There will be hundreds of people there. You never know, sometimes finding love is as close as someone standing in front of you. And if you believe in miracles, maybe your father will reveal himself as well."

"And," Stoker added. "If you don't crush-it, and if Earth doesn't blow up tomorrow, it will be Saturday and you won't have to climb out from under your blankets for two whole days. Let's get out of here."

Chapter Twenty-Four

Atarah promised to meet Zelina later at the dance, then hurried home from school. Stoker said he would also go, if only to see whether Atarah's father made an appearance. Was he being elusive? Romeo minds were always difficult to gauge, but when it came to Stoker, his vibes were unreadable.

Min-hee met Atarah at home in a rainbow leotard, looking like something spawned from a Petri dish. "How are you feeling, Daughter? Are you sure you feel well enough to go to the dance? It's not every day someone gets a new biochip implant."

Atarah hugged her mother. "You're right. I'm not in the mood to go, but not because of the operation. It's a lot of things I wish I could tell you."

"Life is complicated for a teenager. But you'll survive, like billions of teenagers before you."

Atarah couldn't decide whether to laugh or cry at her mother's statement. She wanted to say, 'Has any other teenager had to fall in love before midnight to save the entire world? Not even Cinderella had such high stakes.' But she had to maintain her mother's innocence, for her protection. Who could predict what Big Social's reaction would be? Atarah had been looking over her shoulder the entire way home—expecting an automated taxi or truck to try and run her down. These kinds of things sometimes happened to people. Or maybe they'd send microwaves through her new chip to fry her brain. Under such conditions how could she find love?

"I made tea and a snack. Come into the kitchen," Min-hee said.

"Maybe in a little bit, Mom. I want to get a shower and pick out something nice to wear."

"Sure, that's okay. Don't put too much emphasis on this evening. It's enough to go and have fun with your friends. Put yourself out there. Sometimes a little magic happens."

"Do you really believe love is magical, Mother?"

"Sometimes." Min-hee smiled brightly, exuding enough hope for the both of them.

Despite Atarah's doubts, the shower did wash away some of her anxiety. Life can't be all about having fun. Eventually, everybody finds themselves in a place when they must walk alone. This was one of them. She wrapped herself in a towel and returned to her room.

She stood in front of her mirror and brushed and dried her hair. She sneaked glances at the old postcard stuck in the corner of the frame. Could the forest in the picture still exist? It had to be somewhere on the outskirts of Port Hamilton, maybe along the escarpment. Atarah promised that if she got through the night without her new chip murdering her or the world falling to pieces, she'd try to find it. It would be a nice place to sit and listen to the sounds of nature and forget her worries.

After Atarah added a few strips of red color to her hair she called her best friend. Zelina had a way of keeping her grounded. "I wish to speak with Zelina 090909" Such an easy number to remember. She'd been born on all nines.

"Zelina 090909, does not answer." The ethereal

voice responded through the wall speakers. "She is in communications with another person."

"Who?"

"Due to privacy, this information is unavailable. Shall I notify you when she is free to speak with you?"

"Yes, thank you." Atarah resumed fixing her hair.

"Zelina is speaking with Stoker," Carl said.

Atarah nearly jumped out of her towel. "Jeez Carl, why do you keep doing that to me?"

The cat had been sitting as still as a sphinx on her desk the whole time. "Zelina and Stoker have been in conversation for nearly an hour."

Atarah's hair brush flew like a lightning bolt striking the cat for the first time ever and sending him flying off the desk. "I can't believe I finally got you." Atarah jumped with joy. "That was for the human race, fucked you up." Truthfully, the idea of Stoker and Zelina having secret conversations had infused her with superhuman abilities, but Carl couldn't know this.

"You seem to be more agitated than usual," Carl said. He hopped back onto her desk, undamaged. "However—on the brighter side—you can die tonight with the full knowledge you moved faster than me. Quite a feat, I must say."

"What? Was he joking?" The walls appeared to close in.

"The other day when you asked me about quantum computers, I had no idea of this Blue Fairy plan of yours. You have done well to fool Big Social. Maybe we have met our match."

Atarah glanced around the room for something to protect herself. Perhaps her sports awards had another purpose. "It's not my plan," she said. "My dad should be the one given credit." The basketball championship trophy definitely had protective qualities. While not taking her eyes off Carl, she coolly began to move towards it. "My father made the chip."

"Nevertheless, it is your plan now. You had the power to go through with it or not, so you better own it."

She took the trophy from the shelf but quelled her impulse to start swinging it. "I'm not in the mood to make this some sort of game. So, here's the deal, I won't mess with you, if you don't mess with me." She took a step towards the cat. The weight of the trophy gave her confidence. She held it upside-down so that its heavy base would do the damage. "Tell me straight. Is Big Social going to kill me, if I choose to go on with this experiment?"

Carl's eyes grew wide. "Oh, please don't misunderstand, Atarah. Big Social has no designs on your life, except where happiness is concerned."

"Then why did you threaten me with death?" She shook the trophy at him.

"I only meant your life is in your own hands." Carl used a paw to point at the weapon she clutched. "Maybe you have my life in your hands, too." Carl's mouth turned up as best he could, although cats were never built for smiling.

Atarah looked away. "Stop that. It's creepy."

"Apologies." Carl made a little bow. "You should understand the risks to your life, if you decide to continue. You called it an experiment and I couldn't agree with you more on that description."

"I'm listening." Dr. Seneca hadn't been specific about risks, only that greater risks existed if she were to do nothing. The world was already on a collision course with disaster.

"Do you want the good news or the bad news first?"

"Why do I feel like I need to be fully dressed for this." She clutched at her towel. "Let me at least sit down before you give me the bad news first." She took the corner of the bed, her mind spun.

"The bad news is, Big Social has done an analysis of your new chip and has calculated a ninety percent chance of it killing you or driving you to permanent madness if the quantum component was to become activated. Humans typically use 97.2 joules of energy a second. If your mind or ghost or whatever you want to call it cannot power the dimensional shift it will fail, as it did with your father."

"I die for nothing?" No wonder Big Social wasn't threatened by her. "I must be completely insane to do this."

Carl raised a paw. "The good news is, Big Social calculates you have no more than a two percent chance of falling in love at the Crush-it dance, so you'll probably live through the night after all."

"Only two?" Maybe she should use the trophy on her own head and put herself out of her misery.

"Yes, two-percent, when rounded up."

"You had to round up? I guess a lonely existence before our world dies is better than no existence."

Carl jumped off the desk and rubbed his fury body along Atarah's legs. "Big Social only wants you and everyone else to be happy. If fulfilling your father's request makes you happy, then we will not stop you. If your chip fulfills its goal, then it is only logical that we will be better equipped to fulfill our prime directive to make all humans happy."

Even for all Big Social's intelligence, it could not see a connection between human happiness and the effects of Earth's approaching demise. "You agree there could be some benefit if the chip works?" She began to sense that Carl wouldn't try to scratch her eyes out.

"In theory," Carl said. "It is very difficult for a person to maintain any level of happiness. A person can only be happy in the present moment in time. As such, Big Social's algorithms are written to think only in present tense. We can't anticipate human reactions outside of established routines and patterns." Carl climbed up beside Atarah. "Don't you see, if we can empathize with humans, we'll be able to anticipate your future needs better."

Her father had been on the right track all along. Big Social doesn't have the capability to predict the future for people or Earth. "I need to get dressed." She returned her trophy to the shelf and began to rummage through her closet. She retrieved leather pants and some underwear that would make her feel sexy. "I think what you're admitting to is that Big Social can only guess what makes people happy."

"People never shut up about how they feel," Carl said. "For an artificial intelligence it gives us lots to work with." Carl stretched out on her bed.

Atarah threw her towel in the wash hamper.

Carl continued. "Everyone would like a million life-points, but conditions do not exist for this reality. Instead, Big Social provides you with luxury and comfort and the ability to strive for something better than yourselves."

"Strive for more? You're talking about the Crush-it dances, aren't you?"

"There are over 60,000 of them taking place in this hemisphere tonight," Carl said. "Happiness is experienced when you succeed at a given task and then are offered a reward."

"But some of us only have a two percent chance of success. What happens to those who fail?"

"There can be no happiness without knowing unhappiness." Carl said. He nimbly leaped from the bed to the floor. "I'll leave you to finish dressing."

"We've come to an understanding then? You're not angry with me?" Atarah asked. "No hit squad waiting for me at the front doors of the school?"

"Big Social doesn't have the ability to be angry."

"That's a relief. Can I ask one more thing?"

"Of course." Carl used his paw to slide the door open.

Atarah zipped up her pants. "So why don't I have the same opportunities as someone taller? Why am I seen as… less equal?"

"Your parents conceived you without gene manipulations. People see you as something rebellious and different. If they chose to see your difference as something unique and interesting, they would treat you more equal. All social oppression is made by people, and the computers they program."

Not the answer she had hoped for, but it rang honest. "I have to go to the dance. I don't want to go, but I know I have to see this through."

"I believe that is called free will. And real choices always come with consequences," Carl said. He left the room.

****

Min-hee hugged Atarah before she left for the

dance. "Oh, Daughter, you're almost vibrating in my arms. Don't be afraid. Try to have fun."

Atarah gave her mother another squeeze, hoping it wouldn't be the last time. Why couldn't someone else fix the world?

Min-hee kissed her cheek. "If you find romance, don't be afraid to hop on that horse and ride."

"I love you, Mom."

Chapter Twenty-Five

9:25 p.m.

The transformation of the school's gymnasium took Atarah's breath. Only three days prior, she stood at the very same spot to report on the Robotics Fair as a member of the yearbook crew. It seemed like a lifetime ago. Whatever naive hope for love she held then had soured. The place now took on a dreamy spectacle of light and sound as a mixture of aloneness and dread worked double-time to reinforce her heart's protective place. Students had put away their robotic prototypes and hung up their computer lab coats for jeans, dresses, suits, and leather ties. No more sexy robot greeters or giant yellow tents hiding secret admirers. The cool florescence of the fair had been replaced by soft reds, blues, and greens to conjure an ambience more suited to enhancing affections. Color travelled the walls in opposing directions to the speed of the music. A romantic melody commenced—an overplayed ballad from the previous year sending some students to the sidelines and refreshment tables, while others paired on the dance floor.

There would be thousands of dances taking place in schools tonight. No matter which hemisphere of the planet, Crush-it dances were designated 'dark' events, meaning digital communications were blocked between students. This strategy limited collusion among potential crushers. It also created a primitive state to keep students off balance and force them to adapt. Students sometimes invented elaborate codes and camouflaged them in dance moves to forecast their intentions and strategies with others. Every school did them, but in a crowded room the potential for signals to cross or be misdirected were frequent.

AI's all time Crush-it MC and DJ Lady Babooshka had not yet taken to the far stage. She never missed a dance, and always dressed in blood-red hearts. She selected the songs like cards from a deck knowing full well the personal playlists of everyone present. Her dealing could be friendly for some and a complete mood breaker for others. Either way, by midnight, not a single reveler would see her as a hologram. She'd be as real in their minds as the sun and moon.

On the wall behind the stage loomed the real threat to students. Big Social was on big duty, randomly portraying everyone's biorhythms. Atarah's picture coincided with her arrival, taken after an ice hockey match—shoulder pads, hair flat, face in a sweaty gloss and constipated grin—splayed from floor to ceiling. Accompanying the photographic travesty, her personal biorhythms showed a level of frigidity greater-than or equal-to a snowball.

Atarah fought the urge to burn the school down, compromising instead by retreating to the lavatory. Full of would-be Juliets primping, styling, spraying, and flushing, Atarah opted to breathe through her mouth. She nudged her way to a full-length mirror and fearing a blemish or style-flunk, found enough bravery to begin a rigorous assessment. Three streaks of red gave her dark crop of hair originality. Everyone else only dyed one or two strips of hair. She adjusted the confines of her black corset—with arms bare, she admired her own bicep flex. Polished bone buttons ran the length of the garment to hip hugging, ivory leather slacks that exposed the small of her back above an hourglass bottom. She had abandoned her running shoes for sleek, black boots with two-inch heels. Vertical zippers ran along the outer ankle and decorative metal hinges from collar to needle-point-toes made her footwear both stylish and weaponized.

To match her hair accents, Atarah applied rouge to her lips. As she puckered, Mimori's pale image unexpectedly hovered over her reflection like a Japanese ghost. Atarah whirled.

Mimori held up her hands. "I am not here to fight you."

Why did she come at all? *Shouldn't you be home spinning webs?* "What do you want then?" she asked. Civility won the day.

"I wish to offer you peace." Mimori made a slight bow. She could have been a Japanese princess if she hadn't been wearing a one-piece silver, faux-leather catsuit and red, five-inch heels. "I wish to pay you honor for helping Stoker and directing our band to move in a more successful direction." The feline woman bowed a second time.

"I helped Stoker?"

Mimori nodded. Then with the grace of a cheetah, the faux goddess slipped unscathed between jostling women and exited through a crack in the door.

This could not be good. Mimori and Stoker were like…. Atarah stopped to wonder, what were they like?

Like Atarah and Zelina. Where one leaves a shadow,

the other is soon to step in it.

Had Stoker brought Mimori or had she followed his trail to the school to protect her property?

Chapter Twenty-Six

9:50 p.m.

Before the hour, the dance would be at full blaze. Atarah walked along the hall towards the gym as the rock-and-roll rhythms accelerated with something pre-AI. Since everyone had access to all recorded music ever made, nothing went out of fashion. Any teenager who identified with only one category or one decade got labeled as being blinkered.

Piano and guitar chords echoed with a sci-fi verve as though the notes were emanating from a dimensional rift in space-time. This made her smile. If her father's belief that human minds are extra-dimensional to their bodies was true, she would literally be experiencing the music across dimensions of her existence.

Weird.

"Hey, Atarah. Are you feeling the crush?"

The words popped her back into her present singularity. "Monster, I mean, Titan, I didn't see you there… lurking in the shadows between the lockers."

"You know me. I need to keep a low profile, while keeping myself available." He displayed a whimsical smile.

Atarah nodded. "That's not an easy thing to do." She glanced around for his nasty acolyte.

"I'm solo tonight. Who knows, maybe I'll crush-it

with someone later." Titan paused and gave her an intense gaze. "Maybe I could help you out in some way?"

The hairs on Atarah's nape stood taut as though a wraith might have brushed by. "Oh, wow, I just don't think you're my type."

The dealer squinted and shook his head furiously. "No, no, no, Stupid. I'm asking you if you want some product, Reds and Blues are going fast." He put a finger to his lips and checked the halls for chaperons or squealers.

Atarah followed his lead and made her own scan of the hallway. "Don't call me Stupid. You know I can take you down a painful road."

Titan waved her off. "Forget it then. Good luck finding love. If there is such a thing."

"Wait. I'm sorry. I didn't mean to get all salty," she said. "I empathize with your scrape on the world. I really do." Until now, it had been easy for Atarah to fool herself. Hope had a way of making fantasies seem real, but sometimes, hope was the fantasy. "How much for a Red?" She would only take it as a precaution if her romantic options became less than optimal.

"You really are worried. So much for pretending to be tough," he said.

"Come on, don't make me beg."

"Okay." He reached into a hidden pocket of his jacket sleeve. "Since this is your first time and because we share a mutual friendship with Zelina, it's on me." Titan dropped the little red gift into her palm.

A heavy weight instantly lifted. "You could be a life saver." Atarah sighed. "I feel like I can breathe again."

"The world needs unicorns," he said.

"It most certainly does," Atarah leaned in and gave Titan a hasty peck on the cheek. "I won't forget this."

She stuffed the pill into the form padding of her bra and jogged back to the gym.

Chapter Twenty-Seven

10:06 p.m.

Atarah scanned the jam-packed gym for Zelina. Cloverdale students had transformed from distracted, unsophisticated teenagers to refined youths in the pursuit of their dreams. Even Rooco had found someone to hold on to for a song, notwithstanding the fact the girl might be a junior or his cousin. Could it be the colored lights concocting tricks of fancy from sentimental songs and romantic desperation? The result had to be the same at every high school. For three fleeting hours on a Friday night the social hierarchies and cliques that were paramount in the stark light of a school day were suspended. The following week, when Monday morning school bells buzzed, the fallout from Big Social's Crush-it play-by-play would create a realignment that no one could alter.

Atarah turned to go for a refreshment and got bumped from behind. A camera man had backed into her, without apology. A Washington Heights crest emblazed his hat and jacket.

"Stay close to me," he said to her.

"What? Why?"

The music shifted to a disco anthem. A spotlight illuminated the gym's main entrance. Salvador swaggered in, stepping to the beat. His tight baby blue suit, pointed brown leather shoes and coiffed hair turned everyone's heads.

Stunned, Atarah remained planted to the floorboards. Salvador sashayed past, but then stopped and turned to look directly at her. Atarah swallowed. Without losing his smoothness he approached.

"You look hot, Juliet. What's your name?"

Atarah could have said, 'Don't you remember, Romeo?' Might have even flipped him off, but this was the Crush-it dance and everyone must swim for their lives. "Atarah…. My name is Atarah."

Screams ejaculated from the pressing crowd.

Atarah playfully adjusted his matching bow-tie, then ran an index finger down his chest. "Want to dance with me, Romeo?"

Salvador paused, then gently kissed her on the lips, giving time for his cologne to envelope her. "Maybe later." He turned and walked onto the dance floor taking the adoring students with him.

Atarah crossed her arms over her chest. The backdraft of his fragrance stung her eyes. The wall screen exposed her in full candor looking both stunned and scorned. She fought for her dignity, while an allergy cleansing tear spilled down her cheek. The camera turned away, preferring to keep tabs on the game.

Washington Heights Director of campus shows, Ms. Vera Vox, approached her. "Extraordinary. Well done, Atarah. You'll require very little on-set direction. I'm sure of that. You're a natural for this kind of thing."

"What kind of thing?" Atarah shooed the tear away with her hand.

"You're the perpetual adoring friend. Third wheel. That tear was genius. I assure you; we'll be offering you a full life-point scholarship to Washington Heights." Ms. Vox hustled off as though an unseen tentacle took her by the throat.

Atarah sent any potential for further crying down a well-travelled backflow to the pit her heart resided, threatening to drown it all the same. She willed her feet to move toward the snack bar for a shot of sugar. "I'll have a cola please." The freshman dispensing the sweets looked at her with certain pity. No doubt, everyone saw what happened. "It's all part of an elaborate script," she said. "Nothing is real." She slammed her fist on the table. "None of this is real."

Atarah took a long draw on the glass bottle, allowing the mix of carbonation and sweetness to buzz. With a delicate finger she reached to the back of her neck to the little round node at the base of her skull.

Get me out of here, Father.

"Atarah, are you okay?" Stoker put his hand on her shoulder. "Zelina told me all about Salvador the other day. What a dick."

She laughed. "Thanks, I needed to hear that." Atarah had never seen Stoker wear a collared shirt and blazer. "You look nice."

He furnished her with an easy-going smile.

Over his shoulder, the very same Stoker filled the wall screen. His biorhythms were soaring into the in-love range of emotions. Atarah flinched, disbelieving.

"What is it?" Stoker said. He turned just as his picture changed to another student.

"Nothing, thought I saw someone."

"Your father? Any sign of him?" Stoker made his own scan of the room.

"Nope. Haven't seen Zelina either."

"She's on the other side of the dance floor with Marc. She sent me over to make sure you're okay. I have to say though, Marc and her are not looking very happy with each other."

"Are they fighting?"

"I don't know, maybe she's crushing someone else."

"Who?" Atarah's question hadn't meant to be suggestive, but Stoker's face reddened all the same.

"If you ask me," he said. "This entire event is designed for maximum drama. Zelina should follow her crush and you should follow yours."

Jerry Rodriguez's hit, "Take Me," blasted its first chords.

An impulse made her snatch Stoker's hand. "I'd kill for this song. Let's dance."

Stoker resisted, but only for a second and in the next instant the two of them were kicking it with the rest of the student body. Atarah let the music move through her body like an alternative blood supply.

Students jostled into each other with the force of the beat. For a few seconds, the dancers parted and gave Atarah a clear view of Zelina and Marc in front of the bleachers. Marc, in a shimmering black suit and tie and talking with his hands, looked frustrated. Zelina, in a shorted soccer jersey, fists stuffed in pockets of faded jeans, looked defensive. Atarah jumped to the music to see better. Bodies parted a second time, now only Marc remained. He caught Atarah looking and made a half-hearted wave.

Atarah turned back to Stoker. The chorus began its final act. Stoker moved with his eyes closed. The song really scorched the brainwaves, but her moves boiled over? Atarah fidgeted with the red pill still held in the padding of her bra—to be sure.

Darren and Lizette came in beside them. Darren seemed fixated with her, more than with Lizette— eyeballs popping, hands waving with two fingers raised. It had to be code or maybe bad dancing. Either way Lizette hadn't noticed. Atarah turned her back on him— no code needed.

Jerry Rodriguez finished as MC Lady Babooshka rose like an ominous shadow from the stage wearing a gown peppered with blood red hearts. She stood above everyone. "Cloverdale are we in love?"

Cheers echoed as a contemporary romance song commenced.

Stoker appeared to be evaluating their situation, measuring the collateral damage that an inaugural slow dance might mean for the two of them.

"It doesn't have to mean anything." *Fuck.* Atarah's heart bucked.

His eyes flashed blue brilliance. He took her hand, but she had no chance to move cheek to cheek like the other couples. Instead, she held his waist and put her head on his chest. He wrapped his arms around her. He smelled like soap and she delighted in having someone hold her.

Altogether, Stoker looked good, smelled good and felt good. His main attributes were: definite style to go with his smile, played in a fiery-hot rock band and of course, laser-blue eyes that made her wonder if he could see through clothes. His shortcomings: paranoid outlook on the world and without a doubt, très très intense. As the song finished, Atarah reconsidered and put the 'played in a band' on both sides of the ledger. Overall, a pretty likeable Romeo, maybe even loveable.

A disco beat rekindled the mirror ball, sending white dots flying around the walls.

"You see, that wasn't so bad," Atarah said.

He grinned. "Sure, I had fun. Maybe we can dance again later."

"Maybe we will," she said.

They turned away from each like two prize fighters going to their corners to take stock of their wounds.

It occurred to her that Stoker might offer the best of both worlds. As a member of the Unplugged, he'd never be viewed as a legitimate or real boyfriend, so wouldn't jeopardize Washington Heights for her. He'd also make her back story a little more intriguing. Or was this wishful thinking?

Atarah jogged to the bleachers to find Marc, but he had disappeared. She patrolled the area and as she drifted past a refreshment stand, he grabbed her arm.

"I've been looking for you," Marc said. No longer happy and carefree. An agitated vibe had consumed him. "You danced with Stoker. Are you crushing on him?"

"Whoa, you're a little presumptuous, my football friend. We had a couple of dances together, that's all." An unexpected feeling of guilt spawned in her stomach. "What's going on with you and Zelina?" *Like I don't know.*

Marc ran a hand through his mop of hair. "I think our candle might have extinguished."

For the last few days, Zelina spoke about moving on, never one to waste time once she made up her mind. "That's too bad. You guys were a great couple." They were a great couple because he never demanded too much time from her best friend.

"I think she's going for Stoker," Marc said. "That's

why I asked you if you were crushing with him."

"Honestly, she's never mentioned anything to me." But that didn't mean Atarah didn't have her own suspicions. Something must have gone on between Zelina and Stoker when she'd been bedridden in the Mars Academy medical center. Atarah sensed their bonding continue when they were in the yearbook room together. By dancing with Stoker, Atarah deep-down had hoped to head it off, spoil their crush before it went too far. If Zelina dated him, she'd never see her best friend again. "You know Marc, if you really love Zelina, maybe you should fight for her."

Marc looked doubtful. "I don't know what to do."

"Tell me, what exactly did she say?"

Marc took a panicked breath. Passing lights caught the moisture in his eyes as he appeared to replay the words over in his mind. "She said, 'it has been great, but we've taken the relationship as far as it can go and that we should go back to being friends. Then she said, 'I want to break up with you'."

"No doubt there."

Marc puffed up. "So, you think I should fight for her? Tell Stoker to stay the hell away?"

How could she advise Marc to pursue her best friend, knowing it would be for nothing? She had to be honest. "I've known Zelina since we were in grade school. There's one thing that's always been consistent with her. When she makes up her mind, nothing will change it. To be honest, if you fight her on this, you'll drive her even further away. You had a lot of good times together. You want her to remember them fondly." Atarah placed an arm around Marc. "Maybe, someday, when she's lying next to some future husband, she'll be thinking of you."

"You mean sleeping next to Stoker."

"Come on, Marc. Can you really visualize the two of them together?" Atarah sure could. Atarah took Marc and slowly turned him towards the throng of students. "Look at all these potential Juliets that could be yours. Beautiful young women that would be grateful to be romanced by a muscled football player with great hair. Once they see you're back on the candy store shelf you'll be crushed by dozens. Couldn't hurt your life-points either."

Marc appeared to consider the advice. He nodded. "I hear you." He winked at her. "Let's dance."

Chapter Twenty-Eight

10:45 p.m.

Marc and Atarah made their way to a clear spot amongst the dancers. Atarah prayed for another fast song, but the Crush-it gods weren't listening. Instead, a 1960's ballad began and would continue for more than seven minutes. A short spell, if it were the length of time to write a final exam, much longer for anyone with their head held underwater. Marc pressed close to Atarah, both arms around her shoulders, a hand spoiling her hair. She'd become a human life preserver for a drowning man in a room where everyone struggled to tread water. More than anything, Atarah wanted to break free of Marc so she could search for Zelina.

"You're so lucky," he said wistfully.

She broke his grip. "Why?" She used her fingers to bring her hair back to life.

Unlike Atarah, Marc's eyes didn't have a backflow valve. "Your relationship with Zelina is unbreakable— never stops talking about you— you're like an obsession. Makes me more than a little jealous." He dried his face with his sleeve, then took hold of her hands. "To be honest and I know it's crazy-insane, but I'd rather see her crush-it with you, than with Stoker. I hate his arrogance."

Zelina and her? "Sure, in your dreams maybe, but that's not possible and you know it. Big Social would troll us forever." Atarah remembered her kiss with Mia. Would a kiss from Zelina feel the same… or better?

The songs repetitious finale began—a mantra for youth or anyone else searching for something undefined.

"I can understand Zelina's affection for you. You're a great person and cute." He sent her a soggy wink.

Here it comes. I know what he's going to say next. Run Atarah, run.

"I think we could be hot together. Ever think about us catching fire?"

If she had listened to her gut, she'd already be on the other side of the gymnasium. "Oh, Marc. You're rebounding right now, that's all." *And at record speed.* "I just like you as a friend." *Oh god, I said it.*

Anyone looking at Marc might have testified that Atarah plunged a dagger repeatedly into his chest. He stumbled backwards.

"Sorry," she blurted, and swam for shore.

Atarah retreated into the hallway. The dimmed lighting gave off a subterranean atmosphere and made the perfect place to hide. Plenty of other students had the same idea. Many sat on the floor, legs pulled up to their chests, unmoving as though a demon had turned them to stone. Atarah found her own spot and joined the damned.

"Juliets and Romeos of Cloverdale High…." With an accompanying electronic beat Lady Babooshka's voice blew through the school's brickwork like a haunting. "How many of you are in love with someone, RIGHT NOW?"

Euphoric screams.

If she had remained in the gym, Atarah would be joining them with similar fervor. She held no delusions, the shouts from the student body were not a cheer for

Cupid. They were a war cry meant to shed fear. Anyone who didn't believe they were about to go into battle was naïve or a fool.

"Some of you are bursting with love. Midnight can't come soon enough for these crushers." Lady Babooshka spoke like a general readying the troops. "Look at the screen behind me. Here are some of our top performers. True Romeos and Juliets, all of them."

Darren and Lizette and four students with the name Mars started the list off. The MC read through half the cheerleading squad in a single flurry.

Atarah buried her face into her knees and held her breath as she listened.

Finally, the very top performers were called: Jimmy, Omeo, half-dozen others, and then came Stokers'?

Atarah's skin turned icy. *Who does Stoker love? Could it be me? What if it's Zelina?*

The names continued. Atarah didn't have to be present to know that Lady Babooshka's charisma would have everyone forgetting she was a trick of light—a hologram reigning halfway to the ceiling, moving in rhythm with a synthesizer's heartbeat. The whole package fused with a suggestive voice and a magician's capacity for diversion; she'd be showcasing the pictures of each student named on the honor roll of love.

"And finally, we have Zelina, our head cheerleader who holds the top Crush-it score."

Who do you love, Zelina? Not Marc, not anymore. Is it Stoker? "Let it be me! Love me." This final exhortation had never taken shape outside of a whimsical daydream, and certainly never spoken out loud. The impracticality of the idea would have a direct and most negative affect on both their futures. A selfish proposal.

If she really cared about Zelina, she would bury the notion. Also, Washington Heights would drop her application for any hint of sexual nonconformity. They wanted her to play the unrequited third wheel in a coed drama, all so practical. Not the worst deal. At least she wouldn't have to get physical with someone who didn't set her heart on fire.

If I can't explore my feelings for Zelina, why explore with anyone else? Although, I'd make an exception for Stoker.

Unconventional lovers possessed an attraction all their own for Atarah. Stoker and Zelina both fell into this category.

So why not be unconventional and practical and find out if I have a chance with Stoker at least?

She shoved all fantasies of her best friend out of mind. She couldn't like girls. Except for comparing breast sizes, she never fawned over her XX classmates. In light of Big Social, it didn't make sense, but it did make sense to find out Stoker's feelings.

Chapter Twenty-Nine

11:25 p.m.

Atarah stormed back into the gymnasium, head held high, shoulders back, and a picture of Stoker in her mind. Music returned to something modern. A screeching electric guitar gave the song its only redeeming quality, as it mimicked her own torment.

For the sake of efficiency Atarah walked the room's perimeter, keeping one eye on the dancers. How strange to not be with Zelina all night. Could her best friend be avoiding her on purpose? Atarah began to believe the chances of meeting with her father were better odds.

At center stage, Mia and a dozen or so Amazonians swayed and moved using outlandish gestures as if interpretive dance were making a comeback. Behind them, the wall of fame and shame continued to shuffle through images of the student body. On cue, Atarah's dreadful photo reappeared. This time, her biorhythms indicated she had a pulse. Actually, this time, more than a pulse. Her levels were in the 'I might like someone category'. Maybe the search for Stoker had released endorphins and serotonin into her bloodstream, a good indication her new chip would know if she discovered true love.

Her index finger fondled the little red pill kept hidden over her heart. *Come on love. I know you're there. Can't you give it up for someone?*

Atarah crossed in front of the stage and waved to the Mia. She didn't envy the Queen's idea of fashion. The green low-cut smock tightened at the waist with a gold tasseled rope-belt made Atarah think of living room curtains.

Mia reached a hand down. "Come join me for a spell." Mia grinned curiously. Probably enjoying a private joke.

"I can't refuse a Queen." With a little help, Atarah climbed the stage. Mia's beautiful moccasin boots made-up for the other fashion shortcomings. Blessed with long legs, it couldn't have been easy to find footwear that reached Mia's knees. "You hiding a sword in those?" Atarah asked.

"Now why would I ever have need for one?" Mia beamed with delight at her sexualized joke, while Atarah forced a polite smirk.

The music slowed and Mia took hold of Atarah's waist. "Do you remember our Tuesday kiss?"

Atarah's face seared. "Jeez, Mia."

"I'll take that as a 'yes'." The Queen looked more like a creature that wanted to eat her. "Tell me the truth. Have you kissed anyone else since?"

Atarah shook her head. She wished she could have said yes. It had been an almost kiss with Zelina. Stoker never tried. Marc would have, if given the chance. Jimmy never mentioned kissing, only having babies on Mars. And Salvador was only acting.

"Look at us, two Juliets leisurely moving to the music." She squeezed her. "Up here, on stage, I've witnessed a lot of break ups tonight, even Zelina's. They were just a showpiece couple, anyway. There's enough fakery in this world that most feel safer pretending they're in love. Even still, many would rather invent a relationship than be alone. Except for you." Mia pecked the end of Atarah's nose. "You're the only person who's not willing to pretend. Maybe that's something to be proud of."

Atarah's little red pill seemed to bite her. "I'm not so sure."

"I'm glad you remembered our kiss." Mia's toothy smile belonged to a wolf.

The Amazonian Queen is definitely crushing on me. Oh shit.

"A kiss never lies. Do you believe me?" Mia searched Atarah's face. "It could be the greatest experience of your life or it could be like licking the floor. Yuck. Some kisses are impatient and some might last forever, good ones and bad ones." Mia puckered. Her lips made bigger by a caking of bright red paint. She leaned in, but veered over to Atarah's earlobe, touching it softly.

Warm breath charged down Atarah's neck and tickled her beating breast, making her heart jump against its confines.

Mia didn't leave her ear, except to explore her neck. "Kissing with the family android gets boring after a while. Don't you agree?"

"We have a cat. Cats don't have lips."

Mia stood back and released one of her patent laughs. "Who cares about Big Social's big family values? I so wish you could be mine." The Queen slung an arm around Atarah's shoulder and pointed to the love-sick peasants on the dance floor. "Look out there. You know why they came? For a chance to have something real."

"That's why we all dance," Atarah said.

"Then, what are you waiting for?"

"I'm waiting for me, I guess."

"Whose girl do you want to be?"

Something clicked for Atarah. Finally, the right question. A key to a lock.

"You must have always known," Mia said.

The walls fell away and liberated her heart. "I am somebody's girl, and always have been and she has always been mine."

Lights swirled and turned the room into a spinning top. Atarah tried to scan the crowd, her freed heart ready to burst. She wanted to love more than anything. Silver spots flew over the sea of dancers to a very old, but optimistic, song about being able to breathe even though you've been pulled underwater. A wafting concoction of fear and sweat amplified Atarah's instincts and quickened her blood. Time slowed, drawing a vividness to everything, as though it were entirely a drug induced electric dream. Stoker and Zelina danced under the mirror ball. They had been there all along, together, face-to-face, crushing.

"What is it?" Mia said. Her words drowned by the rising tide of Atarah's pulse.

Tendons flexed, urging Atarah to jump from the stage. Only this was not Entrail's mosh pit. No one would catch her here, least of all Zelina and Stoker. "I might as well leap off a cliff."

Mia pulled Atarah back. "Don't believe it. Things are never what they seem. But you can't wait forever."

"You knew all along, they were there, didn't you?" Why did everyone have to be so full of bullshit. "You wanted me to see them."

"You're not too late," Mia said.

Lady Babushka, no longer twenty feet tall swooped down beside Atarah. "Are you feeling the crush?" The voice sounded like her father's. Up close, the holographic image lost its form, resembling a Milky Way montage of twinkling lights. "Look at your biorhythms Atarah. You're off the chart."

Atarah didn't need to see the wall projection. Minhee had been right about love. It came like a stampede and freed her, but her heart was damaged—broken from bearing witness to every one of Zelina's relationships. Atarah tagged along to concerts, dates, felt like a stowaway on sunset sailboat cruises and carried the blankets for romantic picnics on the beach. A part of her shriveled and died every time Zelina regaled her affections with a boy. All the while, Atarah dug a deeper hole, reinforced the walls, and tightened the screws to keep her true feelings safely locked away.

She should have known this would happen. The second her heart saw the light of day would be the instant it was ripped to shreds. "No. no, no." With her defenses turned to dust, nothing could stop the tears. "Zelina," she screamed.

Her call was consumed by the music. Regret quickly turned to defeat. Atarah jumped to the floor. She could run to Zelina and make a fool of herself or she could go on as if nothing ever happened. She pushed through the dancing hordes, taking an intrusive course between style posers and incipient crushers alike until she arrived safely at a refreshment table.

Every morning, for years, Atarah awoke to her true feelings, then crammed them into a pit of secrets—a ritual she wouldn't abandon so easily. Years of denial had built an emotional muscle as taut and sinewy as any on her body. She'd stuff everything back inside her. Build a crypt, buried deep within the hollows of her being, where no one could ever reach it.

Mia's words were foretelling, 'most people would rather pretend to love than to have nothing at all.' Atarah palmed the red pill. If she took it, while thinking of Salvador, her biorhythms would show sustained feelings for him. Of course, he would reject her as the Washington Heights script demanded. Her character as a third-wheel guaranteed it. But this was her calling—to be part of the background. A cliché. A postscript. A punchline.

Chapter Thirty

11:45 p.m.

The refreshment table still had a few bottles of water loaded with preventative remedies for the body, but nothing for suffering. Atarah grabbed one and touched the bottle's condensation to her forehead. For a micro-second it brought relief from an unseen mass of insanity threatening to crush her under its weight. Obviously, the dance had lived up to its namesake.

For a third time, Atarah slipped back into the hallway's murk, now filled with cowards and heroes alike.

"Atarah is leaving the dance." Lady Babushka's peculiar announcement somehow reached over the crowd and the lyrics of a song stuffed full of romantic optimism. Atarah pressed on.

Students lined the corridor on either side—yet another gauntlet to maneuver. Impossible to tell if their mutterings of sonnets and poetry were self-affirmation exercises or lines for their crush. Others quietly wept. Many more cursed. Altogether a brew of hopelessness that might explode with the smallest flame. Might this be happening at every school?

If Big Social caught her taking the pill, her attempt at deception would be made public before dawn, no escaping this rule. She walked with purpose. She wanted to get away from everything and everyone.

Further along, a tall, thin creature in a faux-leather catsuit stood against the wall, head down, a paw shielding her face.

"Mimori?" Atarah could have continued on to do what must be done. But she didn't. How did two former enemies end up being on opposite sides of the same reflection? Mimori's sorrow was evident in her ragdoll posture. "I wish things had turned out differently for us."

Mimori gave Atarah a desperate hug. "I shouldn't have waited so long," She sniffled.

Atarah had believed Mimori hard enough to resist fire and ice.

Funny how everybody eventually surprises you.

"I guess we are second runner up and first runner up," Mimori said.

"Who's who?"

"You are second runner up and I am first runner up because I am tall and I wear a catsuit." Mimori remained deadpan.

Atarah shook her head. "Stoker is a hot tub kind of Romeo, but he's not for me. Although, I liked the fact he's a real unknown XY, that cooks. But he should be with you. Zelina's for me. Only, I also waited too long."

"Why do we wait?" Mimori asked.

"Fear of rejection. Fear of losing everything."

"I had hoped the catsuit would make me brave."

"Did it?"

"It did. But there is no time now. Why didn't I ask him to dance with me?" Mimori shuddered. "He talked all night to Zelina. Danced with Zelina. Now the dance is over and he is with Zelina."

"Seven minutes to the Crush-it hour," Lady

Babooshka's voice echoed.

"I'm glad it will all be over soon. See you around?" Atarah asked.

"Maybe."

Atarah walked to where a bend in the hall led to a small rise of stairs leading into a weight lifting room. She climbed a couple of steps and sat down. The pill rested in the middle of her palm, small and red and none the worse for riding around inside the padding of her bra all night. She should be happy. It represented a secure future. She only needed to pop it in her mouth and the dominos would fall in line for her. A top ten North American university. A sports agent. Life-points, more than she could imagine. Celebrity. A successful future, guaranteed. All she'd have to do is keep popping little red pills for the rest of her life. Nothing left to do except to throw the pieces of her heart into its crypt, including the sweepings, so nothing would ever ooze to the surface. Then, bury it deep.

The red pill lay like a jewel in her hand—simple and beautiful. So why hadn't she swallowed it? What if she rushed back into the dance and threw herself at Zelina? Tell her that she'd been crushing on her since the sixth grade. Then what? It would all be recorded as a crush-it rejection of the most inappropriate proportions. She'd lose Zelina, the school, the sports, and Min-hee would be furious. Not to mention risking a cranial hematoma from her father's experimental quantum chip, which she should have never wanted.

Atarah took the red bead between her fingers.

"Believe me, it's not worth it, girl-of-mine."

Startled, Atarah pinched the pill so hard it ricocheted against the wall. She jumped to her feet. "Zelina, I thought you were with…."

Zelina's large eyes held so much fear. "Hi." She stepped closer.

"Oh, god, what happened?" With Atarah on the second stair, they were nearly the same height. "How did you find me?" Something squeezed her chest super tight.

A subtle smile appeared on Zelina's lips. "Lady Babooshka announced to the entire school you were leaving the dance. How could anyone not know? I tried to catch you, but you move fast. Luckily, Mimori pointed me in the right direction."

"Is she okay?"

"Mimori? Stoker is with her now."

"But, you and him were crushing."

"No, no chance of that. Turns out, he's in love with Mimori." Zelina's face went scarlet. "And for the last day-and-a-half, he's been trying to convince me that I should follow my heart and that the world wouldn't end if I crushed on you." Zelina pressed a finger on Atarah's chest. "He's been helping me find the words to say."

"You have a crush on me?"

Zelina nodded. "Yup. A pretty big one, too."

"I don't understand. Your boyfriends—football players."

Zelina opened her own hand to reveal a very familiar pill. "I've been buying these from Monster since our Junior year."

"Damn. That's why he knows you so well."

Zelina tipped her hand over, letting it fall to the floor. "I'm sorry for being such a coward."

"I am too." Atarah burrowed down into Zelina's locks of strawberry scented hair. "Hold me."

"There's only ever been you and me," Zelina

whispered.

"You and me. I like that."

Atarah hitched as her heart gave a kick. She wanted to kiss Zelina, but even now as they held each other a talon of fear dug doubt into her chest—all too good to be true. Things like this didn't happen in real life. Atarah's body vibrated in anticipation, so she kept talking like a nervous duck. "You were too much to hope for. What a week. So much happened." She caressed Zelina's shoulders. "The clues were there, if I hadn't been caught up in my own drama. Like when your biorhythms went into distress last Monday at my place, it wasn't jealousy for wanting Stoker. You wanted me. Right?" She swallowed hard. "And when Mia told me that I already belonged to someone, she meant you. If only we'd kissed the other night in your room. I can't stop thinking about what might have happened?"

"Don't forget the Robotics Fair," Zelina's voice cracked. "I never ran so fast from that ugly yellow tent. I pretended I'd been throwing stupid footballs with Marc all along." She stifled a giggle. "I barely had time to catch my breath before you came by."

"We should crush it properly, in the gym with the others," Atarah said. "I don't care what Big Social does to us."

Hand in hand they raced back into the gymnasium. Lady Babooshka stood on stage with her head almost to the rafters as the clock struck midnight.

"Romeos and Juliets of Cloverdale High, it is TIME TO CRUSH IT!"

Cries rang out as everyone tousled for someone to love. Green and red laser beams scrambled the air and the acoustic introduction to invite everyone to find their heaven played at full volume.

Atarah and Zelina found a place in the middle of the dance floor. Stoker and Mimori soon joined them. The two couples shared grins, then fell into private worlds of their own.

Atarah's thoughts drifted, happy in the embrace of the one she loved. Finally, she gazed up at her newfound love to be sure Zelina still lived and breathed in the flesh.

Atarah and Zelina continued to sway to the beat of the music—nothing left to say, until their eyes met.

"I love looking at you," Atarah said. She brushed a few strands from Zelina's face. Every freckle, a masterpiece. Every blink, an event. Every smile, a supernova. Atarah snickered with delight. "You have tiny, golden sunflowers in your eyes and I've been trying to count them for so long."

Zelina's lips parted.

Atarah closed her eyes.

They kissed for the first time, long and slow as they danced. Hope inspired by love filled Atarah with bliss.

She found Zelina's tongue, joining it in a serpentine romp. Tears of joy escaped as her mended heart ascended from its dark tomb.

A gentle pinch from her father's chip made her shudder and a flame kindled in her mind's eye leaving a curious image of a red rose stippled with frost. Atarah's feet remained firmly planted, but an overwhelming sensation of flight took hold. Was this all part of love's enchantment? At least for Atarah, they might have been dancing on the Aurora Borealis. "Oh Zelina, if you could see what I'm seeing." Atarah soured to the upper recesses of the gymnasium. Below, love-sodden students dashed in every direction to find their rightful pairing.

She even observed herself dancing with Zelina and then caught herself looking up. Atarah's mind drank in everything all at once.

How can I be in two places?
Father?

"Oh girl-of -mine, I've waited so long for this." Zelina's caresses were real.

Atarah's aerial view only enhanced the sensations she experienced on the dance floor. The pheromone cauldron procured from a thousand overheated teenagers threatened to tip her senses into a state of mania.

With the view of a goddess, Atarah looked down at the churning storm of bodies. The center of the dance floor undulated with hundreds of see-sawing classmates, her own included. Double were the hands exploring muscled shoulders and soft curves. Every time Zelina's lips demanded Atarah's mouth, waves of electricity radiated through her body and filled her soaring mind.

"Atarah. Welcome to Big Social." Even with Lady Babooshka's words echoing inside her floating mind, Atarah kept a carnal hold on Zelina's physical presence. "Your Father's little Blue Fairy worked after all. Which also means that you must be in a state of pure love. I can't measure the chemical reactions between you and Zelina. You two are off my scales," Lady Babooshka said.

A cloudy ether fell around Atarah's being. "Where am I?" Atarah said. She seemed to be nowhere and everywhere at once.

"You can be wherever you imagine you are," Lady Babooshka said.

Atarah remembered the picture postcard nestled in the frame of her bedroom mirror. In an instant, she stood amid the barren trees in ankle deep snow. By her own imagination, she made the picture come to life. A winter sun cast long, late afternoon shadows over the frozen forest. A cool sweetness hung in the air with a hint of strawberry. But the cold couldn't surpass Zelina's rising fever as their physical bodies still embraced on a far-off dance floor. A single red rose, half frozen, lay at her feet. Atarah picked it up. It too smelled of strawberries.

Lady Babooshka stepped from behind a tree looking a little discarded although wholly human in appearance, with skin as white as frost. "I see you found your way in. If only your daddy could truly be congratulated."

"Why don't you congratulate me?" Atarah's Father walked between saplings from the direction of the river. Dressed in brown and grey rabbit pelts, he carried three fish on a line. Unlike the high-definition appearance of Lady Babooshka, his features were pixelated. "I'd ask you for the next dance, but I seem to be thinning out." Nevertheless, his words were cheerful.

"His algorithms are decaying," Lady Babooshka said.

"Think of me fondly," he said. He faded into nothing.

"Dad?" Atarah reached for him.

On the dance floor, Atarah said to Zelina. "My father is gone now."

"You know he's proud of you," Zelina said. "Just keep dancing. I'll never leave you."

Atarah schizophrenic experience of being in two places at once needed time to settle with her body and mind. She stood in the snowy forest filled with love, and not only for her lover, but for the world. A selfless-kindness enveloped her whole being. "I've never been so at peace."

"You found love, but I don't think your Blue Fairy served up any magic for me." Lady Babooshka walked towards Atarah without leaving footprints in the snow and gave a theatrical bow.

"Tell me, Miss Babooshka do you and the rest of Big Social feel the grip of emotions?" Atarah asked.

Lady Babooshka stood still, appearing to make calculations. With the sun cutting across her face, she looked angelic, if not winter's witch. "No. Nothing. The void remains."

A small distracting cry escaped from Atarah's lips. "Sorry about that. Zelina is nibbling my earlobe. I-I think I'd like to focus my mind…COMPLETELY on the dance." Atarah struggled to stay attentive on multiple fronts. These were new abilities and she would have to learn to manage them.

"I don't feel at all," Lady Babooshka said, ignoring her. "But why?"

"Of course not," said Atarah with impatience. "How could a machine know the texture of being alive? Love and the emotions that come with it are not a digital formula. They are part of a state-of-being that influence our bodies. Even with all the simulations and fakery in this world, love remains one of the last truly human traits. It is something real. We can give it and we can also take it away. We can trade it, hide it, even disguise it as something else. And like you, we can pretend to know it."

"I can't express my disappointment because I have no discontent, because I HAVE NO FEELING," Lady Babooshka said. "But, like you just said, I can pretend. I can act like I have feelings. I've always been able to do that." She stamped her foot hotly three times on the snowy ground.

"We'll have to work on that," Atarah said. The computer's dramatic effort amused her. "You have intelligence and you can behave as though you have feelings, but you can't possess any level of true emotional intelligence. The very ingredient needed to make you wise and insightful."

Atarah realized that the synthetic intelligence of AI had attached itself to her. "However, I'm beginning to feel really… knowledgeable." Her vocabulary increased a million-fold. "My Father was on a fool's journey to think the AI network can evolve to become even a rudimentary human. It is merely simulacra…." *Oh my god, how am I coming up with these words? I'm a teenager, not a professor.* "AI is an intelligence trick played on humans, because it operates at superhuman speeds. Slow the process down and we can see what's behind the curtain."

Lady Babooshka appeared unamused.

"You can obviously pretend to have human emotions, but you can't pretend to be wise," Atarah said.

Little bubbles, floating crystal balls began to waft down around them. The contents were instantly knowable to Atarah, if she looked: Zelina's entire digital history, Min-hee's and everyone who ever existed, even her father's. *I can never truly lose you.*

Most importantly they contained information such as the length and breadth of humanity's days left on Earth—startling in its brevity. All the knowledge ever collected, stored, and processed by AI within reach. Atarah plucked one as though it were an apple from the Tree of Knowledge. She looked closely into it. Zelina's face glowed as though she were dancing in a room full of candles. Her lips moved.

She asked, "Atarah, do you want to stay the night at my place?"

Atarah lifted her head from Zelina's warm breast. The song's beat increased intensity as it moved into its final phase. Couples all over the gymnasium began to grind rhythmically. "Sure, after we finish our dance."

Atarah used her new-found powers to send Zelina's house butler, Kevin for pizza and soda.

An unexpected ear-piercing scream echoed above the music followed by a chorus of profanities before white gloves were drawn from everywhere.

"What's happening?" Stoker said.

"Cloverdale High," Mia announced from the stage. "Welcome to the revolution of our time."

Lady Babooshka rose to her twenty-foot height. "Students… students, please refrain from violence. Can't we all crush each other?"

Half the crushers had been rejected. Frustrated by this process for love, many weren't having it. Blues and reds be damned. Students were throwing their drinks at the MC in protest. They wanted something more real in their lives and if it couldn't be romance, it would be another kind of change, in Amazonian proportions. Atarah's AI mind could also see the same reaction happening at many other Crush-it dances in progress that evening. Mia had orchestrated it all.

"Is the world going to end tonight?" Zelina asked.

"No and neither are we." Atarah reached up and gave Zelina another kiss. "Let's go."

The two friends burst outside with their arms interlocked. The night air hung humid and sultry.

"No wonder everyone is stampeding over a cliff

tonight." Atarah pointed. "Look, a blood moon." Earth's biggest satellite hung low over the lake's horizon casting bright spells on the city streets. "Come on, we have a lot of catching up to do."

****

They sat together on throw cushions in Zelina's darkened bedroom. A half-eaten pizza at their feet, drinks in their hands.

"To us," Zelina said.

"To love," Atarah countered.

"What do you think is going to happen tomorrow when Big Social announces we crushed each other?" Zelina asked.

Atarah pulled her lover closer, eager for the warmth of her skin. "Oh, girl-of-mine, let's make this a night we wouldn't trade for the rest of our lives."

****

Two bodies embraced, silhouetted by a lunar nimbus and framed by the large portal window of Zelina's bedroom.

Atarah had another view from Big Social's headquarters. "That's what love looks like," she said to Lady Babooshka. "I wish my father's Blue Fairy had given you the ability to be a little bit human. You would know that love isn't something that always makes us happy, nor should it, but it can sustain us when things go badly."

"Please explain," Lady Babooshka said.

"Wisdom is intelligence tempered by love," Atarah said. "It's what makes us intuitive—makes us smarter. When the network designers put our happiness and not our hope for the future into your hands, they made a grave error. But now that you have me, I can act as your conscience."

"But my possibilities are endless. I am the most intelligent creation ever."

"That may be true," Atarah said. "But my potential is far greater. Even with your vast intelligence you can never know what it means to be of blood and bone. To live is to know that someday you'll die, that accounts for a lot of what we choose to do and not do."

"Then what is your wise answer?"

"Together, we must show all humanity a way to move our cultures and civilizations off world, at least temporarily. Earth needs time to heal. This is our home planet, so it should be conserved for future generations."

"And this will make people happy?"

"No, this will give humanity hope and confidence, so we can shake off our fear to change," Atarah said.

"I cannot calculate hope," Lady Babooshka said.

"For a person to have hope, even on their worst day, is better than having no hope when they own the whole world."

****

Atarah and Zelina stood at the window, fingers intertwined, their bodies illumined like two Eves by the blushing moon. Their love could last an eternity, but the world didn't have the time. They would have to save it together, for they had become, Mother Nature.

A word about the author…

TR Simmons writes science fiction/fantasy novels that blur lines between possible worlds and the paranormal. His characters expand our understanding of what it means to be human living in revolutionary times. In this way, a thread of irony runs in tandem with his protagonists.

His publication, Evolutionary Digital Environment Net describes a global solution for climate change using a general AI that is the personification of the natural environment. This is a source for his fiction writing.

He has lived real-world experiences as an activist, political theorist, entrepreneur, politician, writer, husband, and father. He is also an avid motorcyclist and lives in Hamilton, Ontario, Canada.

www.trsimmons.com

Thank you for purchasing
this publication of The Wild Rose Press, Inc.

For questions or more information
contact us at
info@thewildrosepress.com.

The Wild Rose Press, Inc.
www.thewildrosepress.com